DEAD-EYE SHOT

"Don't let him shoot no more," Emory said. He raised his hand to touch his ear and see if it was still there, then turned to look at the bullet hole in the wall. Sweat was running down his face, soaking his shirt beneath his arms.

"You ready to talk, Emory?" Clint asked.

"I—I need a beer," Emory said. "Then I'll tell ya what ya want to know."

"Okay," Clint said, "get yourself a beer."

While the old man went behind the bar for a beer, Clint touched Barton's arm and moved him back to the table.

"Look out!" Barton shouted.

He turned, put his left arm out, and pushed Clint away from him violently. Clint, falling to the floor, watched as the blind man drew his gun and fired toward the bar.

Behind the bar Emory stood with a gun. Barton fired three times, and two bullets struck Emory, driving him back against the shelves of liquor. . . .

The Gunsmith *series*

J. R. Roberts

Books 127 – 189

For books 1 - 126 go to:
www.speakingvolumes.us

THE GUNSMITH

#147

BLIND JUSTICE

SPEAKING VOLUMES, LLC
NAPLES, FLORIDA
2017

THE GUNSMITH
#147 BLIND JUSTICE

ISBN 978-1-61232-750-1

THE GUNSMITH

#147

BLIND JUSTICE

J.R. ROBERTS

Chapter One

Clint Adams felt the same feeling of anticipation every time he entered a new town. True, most small Western towns were alike, but there was still that unknown quantity. Who would he meet? What would the people be like? Would he find a good place to stay, a good place to eat?

There was a time in his life when that anticipation was gone, when he didn't feel any kind of enthusiasm for new places and new people. That happened sometime in his thirties, but now that he was older he realized that if you approached every day and every situation with enthusiasm, then every day could be an adventure in your life. Since coming to that realization, one day had never seemed quite like the one before to him.

As towns went, Liberty, Wyoming, was somewhere in the middle. Not exactly a small town, it was still not quite as booming as places like Dodge City or Tombstone. Still, it had more than one street with a real name, and it had two hotels and two saloons. Any town with two of either had at least a variety of things to offer, but a

1

town with two of *each*—well, that was a town with room to grow. If a town needed two saloons and/or two hotels, there was always the possibility that it would someday need more.

He directed his rig down Liberty's main street, watching the people he was passing on either side. All of the storefronts were open and operating, not a single one boarded up. Closed-down storefronts were a sure sign that a town was fading. There didn't appear to be any danger of that here in Liberty.

Pedestrians in the street or on the boardwalk gave him some attention as he rode by, a curious glance or two. Others who were involved with their work did not look up. That told him that it was not unusual for strangers to ride into town.

He passed the sheriff's office, which was a sturdy-looking, one-story structure with a shingle hanging next to the door. The fact that there was a shingle usually meant that the resident lawman either had been there awhile or intended to be.

He also passed a couple of small cafés, and he was sure that each of the hotels would have a dining room. There would be no shortage of places to eat.

Finally, he came to the livery, which was a large building in good condition with a corral on the side. Inside the corral were a few decent-looking horses.

As he called his team to a halt and put on the brake, a man came walking out of the livery, wiping his hands on a rag. He was hatless and sweating through his shirt. There were big, wet half-moon stains beneath his arms, and his shirt was open in front to show a glistening, solid, hairless chest. The man appeared to be well over six feet, probably in his mid-thirties, not only a liveryman, but obviously a blacksmith as well.

"Afternoon," he greeted as Clint stepped down. Once he was on the ground, Clint could see that the man was about six three or four.

"Good afternoon," Clint said. "I'm looking to put up my horses and put my rig someplace."

"Got room inside for your horses," the man said. "Some space out back for your rig. Gonna cost you, though."

"Naturally," Clint said amiably. "I didn't intend to take up your space for free."

"Well, drive the rig around back, then," the man said. "I'll unhitch your team and tend to them."

"Got a big, black gelding tethered to the back," Clint said. "He gets tended to first."

The man walked to the rear of the rig and gave Duke a long, admiring glance.

"I can see why," he said finally. "Fine-looking animal."

"Yes, he is."

"Biggest bastard I ever seen," the man said, shaking his head. "What's his name?"

"What makes you think he's got a name?"

The man smiled for the first time, revealing that he was missing one of his front teeth.

"You said *he* instead of *it*," he said. "Man who talks about a horse that way generally names him. Am I right?"

"You're right," Clint said. "His name's Duke."

"Duke," the man repeated. "That fits him."

"You look like you're busy," Clint said. "I could unhitch the team and walk all three horses inside, if you like."

The man waved his offer away.

"Nah," he said, "I'm always busy, that ain't ever gonna change, thank the Lord. I'll take care of them. I just need you to drive your rig on back."

"Okay," Clint said.

The man went back inside. Clint climbed aboard his rig, released the brake, and drove it behind the building, where he found the man standing. He stepped down, then walked to the rear of his rig and removed his saddlebags and rifle to take with him to the hotel.

"Gonna be in town awhile?" the man asked.

"Might be," Clint said. "Couple of days, anyway."

The man peered into the back of the rig while he untied Duke.

"Gunsmith?"

"What?" Clint asked. He wondered if the man had recognized him.

"I asked if you was a gunsmith," the man said. "Seems like it, from the looks of your rig."

"Oh, yeah," Clint said. "I do some gunsmithing."

"Might be some work available in town."

"I just might be interested."

"My name's Bill Adler," the man said.

"Clint Adams. What am I going to owe you for this?"

"Don't know," the man said, scratching his head. "I'll figure out a fair price, though, and you can pay me when you leave."

"Sounds good to me," Clint said. "Any recommendation about which hotel to stay in?"

"Nope," the man said. "They're both about the same if you're worried about your room."

"What about food?"

"Plenty of places to eat in town," Adler said. "The Liberty House has the better dining room of the two hotels, though."

"Much obliged for the information," Clint said.

"The saloons are about the same, too, if you're worried about beer or whiskey," Adler said.

"And girls?"

Adler smiled.

"Both got pretty girls."

"What about gambling?"

"That'd be the Broken Wheel Saloon," Adler said. "They got some game tables in there. You want to gamble in the Red Saddle, you got to find your own game."

"Well," Clint said, "you've been real helpful. Everybody in town as helpful as you?"

"It's a friendly town, Mr. Adams," Adler said, "providing you're friendly yourself."

"That can be said for most towns, I guess," Clint said. "Towns are generally what you make of them."

"I'll take real good care of Duke, here," Adler said, "and your team."

"Thanks," Clint said. "I'll stop in later and check on him."

"Sure thing," Adler said. "Come on, big boy, let's go inside."

Clint watched as Bill Adler walked Duke into the livery, and the big, black gelding followed behind him docilely. He thought that the two were probably going to get along very well. It was rare that someone handled Duke that easily. The horse probably felt that he could trust the man. Also, Adler was big enough not to be intimidated by the horse.

Clint hoisted his saddlebags up onto his shoulder and headed for the hotel.

Chapter Two

Clint Adams was in his hotel room when the two men rode down the street, just about twenty minutes after he did. Even in Liberty where strangers were a common sight, it was unusual for new arrivals to ride in that closely together in time. These two men also attracted more attention than Clint had because one of them was an Indian. The other, a white man, sat his horse stiffly and stared straight ahead. To some, it even seemed that the Indian, riding just ahead of the white man, was actually leading his horse.

Instead of looking for the livery, they stopped at the first hotel they came to, which was not the one Clint Adams had checked into. This one was called the Doubletree Hotel.

The Indian dismounted first, then turned to assist the white man in doing so.

"I can do it, Running Deer," the man said. "I can still get down off a horse without falling."

John Running Deer took no offense at the tone in Stan Barton's voice. He'd been hearing it for the past month, and was used to it by now.

7

"Let's go inside," he said.

John Running Deer was a full-blooded Blackfoot Indian who had been educated as a young man in the ways of the white man. Consequently, he spoke flawless English. He did, however, wear the buckskin and moccasins of his people, as well as the headband and long hair. Although he probably could have passed for a white man in word and manner, he chose not to do so. He was proud of his heritage, and dared anyone to comment about it. It was as plain as day in the cast of his face and the color of his skin.

John Running Deer worked for Stan Barton in a very unusual capacity.

He was the man's eyes.

They entered the hotel, with Running Deer walking right next to Barton. He had his hand on the man's elbow, although anyone watching might well have missed that fact. It seemed, for all intents and purposes, as if the two men were simply walking side by side. Over the Indian's left arm were the saddlebags from both men's horses. The white man was carrying his own rifle. The Indian had left his rifle on his horse.

As they approached the front desk, the clerk looked up and was taken aback. First, the last thing he expected to see was an Indian in the hotel, and secondly he found the look on the white man's face unsettling. His eyes were blank and seemed to be staring right through him.

"Can I help you?" he asked.

"A room," Barton said.

"Uh, we don't rent rooms to Indians here," the man said nervously.

"He's not staying," Barton said. "The room is just for me. My friend will make his own arrangements."

"Very well," the clerk said. He turned the register around and said, "Please, sign in."

He was surprised when the Indian picked up the pen, dipped it in the inkwell, and signed the book. When the Indian was done, the clerk turned the book around and read the name he had written: *Stan Barton*.

"You want a room overlooking the street, Mr. Barton?" the clerk asked.

"It doesn't matter," Barton said.

"Good view from the front of the hotel—"

"I don't use the window," Barton said.

The clerk frowned, and that was when he realized *why* the man seemed to be looking through him.

He was blind!

"Uh, all right, then," he said. "I'll give you number five."

"Fine."

The clerk held the key out, and the Indian took it from him.

"I'll just walk him up," John Running Deer said.

"Oh, all right," the clerk said.

As they walked away from him and started up the stairs, the clerk thought them a strange pair. But then he noticed something even stranger.

Why would a blind man be wearing a gun?

Chapter Three

John Running Deer left Stan Barton in his hotel room, resting on the bed. He went back downstairs, ignoring the stares of the desk clerk, and strode outside. There he mounted his horse and led Barton's horse behind him until he found his way to the livery.

Bill Adler heard the sound of two horses approaching. He had just finished rubbing down Clint Adams's team, having already taken care of Duke. He dropped the grooming brush he'd been using to the ground and walked outside. He was surprised to see an Indian sitting a horse and leading a second. Both horses wore saddles.

"Can I help you?"

"I'd like to put up these two horses . . . please," Running Deer said.

"Sure thing," Adler said. "Step on down and I'll take them from you."

John Running Deer stepped down, and Adler saw that he was wearing a six-gun, like a white man. He watched as the Indian removed his rifle from its scabbard.

Adler noticed that the brave was a good size, probably only an inch or so shorter than himself, but equally impressive through his arms and chest. He found it hard to guess an Indian's age, but since the man's hair had some gray in it he figured him for early forties.

"How much?" the Indian asked.

"How many days?"

"One," the Indian said, with an impassive shrug, "maybe two."

"You can pay me when you leave."

"I'd rather pay in advance," the Indian said.

"Fine," Adler said. He named a figure, and the Indian paid it without argument. It had been a fair figure. He would need to give the Indian change, though.

"I'll have to go inside to get change."

"I'll walk them in," the Indian said.

"Fine," Adler said.

He entered the livery, with the Indian behind him leading the two horses. Adler noticed that both horses seemed worn-out.

He went into his office to get the Indian's change, and when he came out he found the brave examining Clint Adams's gelding, Duke, but from outside the stall.

"I wouldn't get too close," Adler said. "He can get kind of ornery."

Even though the gelding had cooperated with him, the liveryman knew horses.

"How much?"

"What?"

"How much for the gelding?"

"He ain't mine to sell."

"Whose is he?"

"Belongs to a man who just rode into town about half an hour ago."

"Who is this man?"

"Said his name was Adams," Adler answered, "Clint Adams."

"Will he sell it?"

"I doubt it."

"Where is he staying?"

"Liberty House, I think."

"If you see him," Running Deer said, "tell him I want to buy the horse."

"I got other horses outside," Adler said.

"Yes," Running Deer said, "I'll need two, but I want this one."

"I'll tell him," Adler said, "but I doubt that he'll sell him."

Running Deer looked at Adler. His face held no expression.

"For the right price," he said slowly, "anything is for sale."

With that the Indian turned and walked out. Absently, Adler reached out and stroked Duke's nose. The Indian seemed determined to buy the gelding. He sure would like to be around when Clint Adams told him no.

Chapter Four

In his room Clint Adams had removed his boots, hung his gun belt over the bedpost, and sat on the bed. He'd had no intention of sleeping, but he'd drifted off while leaning against the headboard. He came to with a start and looked around quickly. There'd been a time when he never would have drifted off to sleep unwillingly, and when he always woke instantly alert. He rubbed his face and checked the time. He'd napped for about forty minutes.

He swung his feet to the floor and rubbed his face with his hands. Driving the rig always seemed to tire him out more than just riding the trail on Duke's back. Also, the rig's seat seemed to be harder on his tail than his saddle was.

He stood up and walked over to a table with a basin and a pitcher of water. He poured some water into the basin, then removed his shirt and washed up. He used the dirty shirt to dry off, then took a clean one from his saddlebags and put it on.

He licked his dry lips and figured he'd get a beer even before he went to get something to eat. He left the room and went downstairs.

As Clint left the Liberty House Hotel he saw a man walking across the street. He stopped and looked on curiously because the man was an Indian. Also, he was wearing a side arm and carrying a rifle. The rifle wasn't strange, but it was unusual for an Indian to be wearing a holstered firearm.

He watched—as did others—as the man walked on until he reached the other hotel. When the Indian went inside, Clint turned away and started down the street.

As John Running Deer reentered the hotel, the clerk looked up and widened his eyes. Was the Indian going to demand a room after all?

The Indian stopped at the desk and stared at the nervous clerk.

"Can I, uh, help you?"

"Is there a rooming house in town that would give a room to an Indian?" he asked.

The clerk couldn't get over it. The man looked like a savage, but he talked just like a white man.

"Uh, yeah, there is," he said finally. "At the north end of town, a big, yellow, two-story house. It's run by a woman named Molly Mulligan."

"Thank you," the Indian said. He started away, then turned and said to the clerk, "I'll just go up and check on my . . . friend."

"Uh, sure," the clerk said, and watched as John Running Deer mounted the stairs.

•   •   •

Upstairs Running Deer knocked and waited until Barton found his way to the door and opened it. It would have been easier to have left it unlocked, but as an ex-lawman Barton had gotten into the habit of locking his doors.

"Got the animals taken care of?" Barton asked, groping his way back to the bed. His gun belt was hanging on the bedpost, and his hat was on the floor next to the bed. In fact, he stepped on the hat as he sat on the bed and then kicked it away from him in annoyance.

Running Deer walked across the room and picked up the hat.

"Yes, they're taken care of," he said.

"Got yourself a room?"

"Not yet," the Indian said. "I wanted to check on you first."

"Well, I'm fine," Barton said. "I'll just sit here like a tree stump while you get yourself a room, and then we can go and get something to eat."

Running Deer hung the hat on one of the bedposts.

"I thought you were all through with the self-pity, Stan," he said.

Barton rubbed his face, looked annoyed, and said, "So did I, John. I guess it'll take a little longer than I figured. I'm sorry I snapped at you."

"Forget it."

"Go on," Barton said, "get yourself a room and then come back."

"All right."

"Oh, what about fresh horses?"

"The liveryman has some for sale," Running Deer said. "In fact, I have my eye on one."

"All right," Barton said. "We can do that after we eat."

"Or tomorrow," Running Deer said. "There's no hurry."

"That's easy for you to say," Barton said, but Running Deer ignored the remark.

"There's a rooming house in town that will give me a room," Running Deer said. "I should be back soon."

"I'll be here," Barton said, lifting his feet onto the bed and pressing his back against the head-board. "Right here."

Chapter Five

Clint walked over to the Broken Wheel Saloon. Above the door was a big cracked—or broken—wagon wheel. Clint wondered if there was a story behind that. Probably. There was usually a story behind most things.

He entered and saw that the place was far from being in full swing. It was too early in the day. The gaming tables were still covered with green cloths. There were, however, a couple of girls working the room, and he saw that they were both very pretty. One was a blonde in her early twenties, her hair worn piled up on her head to show off her long, graceful neck. She was very slender, with long, lithe legs. The other was a full-bodied brunette with enough cleavage for both girls, and then some. In a few years she might even be called chubby, but right now—in her late twenties—she was still extremely pleasing to the eye of any man who liked his women . . . round. She had big, round breasts and round hips, and a little round chin. Her eyes were big and a pretty dark brown.

17

Clint walked to the bar, where three men were standing almost evenly spaced from each other. He stood at the far end of the bar, which placed him as evenly spaced as the rest of them. They were all ignoring each other, and he followed suit.

"Help ya?" the bartender asked.

"A beer."

"Sure."

The bartender drew the beer and placed it in front of him.

Four of the tables had men seated at them, two hosting single men, two men sitting at a third, and three men at a fourth. One of the girls—the blonde—was standing at the table with the three men, her hand on one man's shoulder. She was speaking earnestly to all three.

The brunette was talking to one of the men who was alone, then she turned and walked to the bar. She bypassed the other three men, probably because she had spoken with them already, and walked to Clint since he was the newest man in the room.

"Howdy," she said, smiling.

"Hello."

"Just get into town?"

"About an hour ago."

"Looking for some action?"

"There doesn't seem to be much around this early," he said.

She put her hand on his arm.

"Not down here, maybe," she said, "but there could be some upstairs."

He doubted that she was telling him there was a poker game upstairs.

"In your room, maybe?"

She wet her bottom lip with her tongue and said, "Yeah, maybe."

He smiled back at her and said, "I'm tempted, darlin', but my guess is that you'd want to get paid for your services."

She pouted and said, "Somethin' wrong with a girl wantin' to get paid for her work?"

"Nothing at all," he said, "but I never did think of going to bed with a woman as work."

"Well, it won't be," she said, "not for you."

"Well, I don't want the woman with me thinking of it as work either."

"I won't then," she said, shrugging her round shoulders. "If you pay me enough."

"Sorry," he said, shaking his head. "I think I'll wait for the action down here to start."

"What about my girlfriend?" she asked, jerking her chin in the direction of the blonde. "Maybe you like skinny blondes better?"

"I like women in all shapes and sizes."

She put her hands on her hips and said, "You just don't like to pay for a poke?"

"That's right."

She eyed him speculatively and then said, "You don't look like a cheapskate."

"I'm not."

"Then that means you think you're that good in bed?" she asked.

He laughed.

"I guess that depends on the woman with me, doesn't it?"

"Mister," she said, swaying from side to side with her hands still on her hips, "you're makin' me almost curious enough."

"Curious enough for what?"

"To give you a free ride," she said, "which no self-respectin' workin' girl would ever do."

"What's your name?" he asked.

"Betty."

"Well, Betty," he said, "I wouldn't want to be the cause of you losing any of your self-respect."

She moved closer to him so that her plump breasts brushed against him.

"You sure I can't change your mind?"

"I'm sure if anyone could, it would be you," he said, "but not today."

"Well," she said, "for as long as you're in town, maybe I'll just keep tryin'."

"No harm in trying."

"What's your name, honey?"

"Clint."

"I'll be seein' you around, Clint."

"I'm sure you will, Betty."

He watched as she walked over to the blonde, tapped her on the shoulder, and started talking to her. The way they were both casting their eyes his way he was sure he was the topic of conversation.

"What time do the cloths come off the tables?" he asked the bartender.

"In about an hour," the man said, "or whenever the dealers show up. They should be comin' in anytime now to set up their tables. You want another beer while you're waitin'?"

Clint put his empty mug down and said, "No, I think I'll get something to eat and then come back."

"Suit yourself," the bartender said with a shrug and moved to the other end of the bar.

Clint looked over at the two girls again, who seemed to have lost interest in him by this time, and then he turned and left.

Once outside, instead of looking for someplace to eat right away he decided to walk over to the livery and check on Duke. His instinct about men and horses was usually good, but he was curious about how Bill Adler and Duke were getting along.

Chapter Six

John Running Deer went up to the front door of the rooming house and knocked. The woman who opened it was redheaded, probably in her early thirties, and she smelled like she'd been working. She was sweating, and the scent of her drifted into the Indian's nostrils. She was attractive, even with her hair flying about.

"And what can I be doin' for you?" she asked in an Irish lilt.

"I understand you rent rooms to Indians."

"I rent rooms to anyone who can pay," she said, eyeing him. "Can you pay?"

"I can pay."

"Then come in."

She moved aside to let him pass, and in brushing past her the sharp scent of her perspiration was even more noticeable. John Running Deer had nothing whatsoever against white women, and he found this one very pleasing. He wondered how she felt about Indians.

"You'll have to excuse the way I look," she said, then wrinkled her nose and added, "and smell, but I've been cleaning the place. I keep a clean place."

"I'm sure you do."

She closed the door and ushered him into the house ahead of her.

"This is the living room; it's available to anyone who wants to sit. In there is the dining room. Meals are at eight, one, and six. Can you make that?"

"I'll manage."

"How long will you be here?"

"Probably only a day or two."

"Well then, there's no need for you to memorize a schedule, is there?"

"No, ma'am."

"Don't *ma'am* me," she said. "My name's Molly."

"Molly."

"And you?"

"John."

She looked at him curiously then said, "You talk like a white man, and you've got a white name?"

"My name is John Running Deer."

She smiled and said, "That's real pretty."

"Thank you."

"I assume you were turned away at the hotels?" she asked.

"I only tried one," he said. "I figured the other would be just as bad."

"It would," she said. "Are you here alone?"

"I'm with a friend."

"Friend?" Her look was still curious.

"A man," he said. "He's at the hotel, the Doubletree Hotel. I . . . work for him."

"Doing what?"

"Just . . . traveling with him."

"As a bodyguard or something?" she asked.

Running Deer decided that was as good a description as any for what he did, although Barton would never have agreed with it.

"Something like that."

"I see," she said. "Well, let me show you to your room so I can get on with my cleanin'. Follow me upstairs, please?"

"Yes, ma—I mean, Molly."

"I can't guarantee how the other boarders will like you being an Indian."

"That's all right," Running Deer said. "I can take care of myself."

She was on the third step while he had yet to start up, and she turned to look at him, taking in the size of him very deliberately.

"Yes," she said, "I'd just bet that you can."

He followed along behind her, acutely aware of her bottom, which was at eye level as she ascended the stairs ahead of him, and of her aroma trailing along behind her. He found both very pleasing.

He wondered again what she thought of Indian men.

Chapter Seven

When Clint reached the livery, he walked in and found Bill Adler sitting on a bale of hay, eating a sandwich.

"Time for a break, huh?" Clint asked.

"Ha," Adler said, "you caught me."

The liveryman also had a glass of cold lemonade on the ground by his foot. He picked it up now and drank from it.

"Looks good."

"Comes from the Golden Palace Café," Adler said. "Down the street a couple of blocks. It's run by a widow who's sort of sweet on me."

"And you on her?"

"Well . . . maybe," Adler said with a bashful shrug. "You come to check on your horse?"

"Just curious how you two are getting along," Clint said.

Adler stuck his sandwich in his mouth so that both hands were free and wiggled his fingers.

"Still got all my fingers," he said, taking the sandwich out of his mouth. "We're gettin' along just fine. He's got a sweet disposition."

"Duke?"

"That's who we're talkin' about," Adler said.

Clint walked over to the stall where the big gelding was. He patted Duke's massive neck and spoke to him softly for a few seconds. The big horse looked completely content with his treatment.

"He looks good," Clint said.

"You can take more credit for that than I can," Adler said. "I didn't raise him, I just rubbed him down."

"I didn't raise him," Clint confessed, "but I've had him a long time."

"Well, you've obviously treated him right."

"Mistreated him on occasion, but he just shrugs it off."

"Well, he looks good enough for somebody to be interested in buying him."

Clint frowned.

"You talking about someone specific?"

"Yeah," Adler said. "An Indian came in not long after you did."

"An Indian? Wearing a gun belt?"

"Yeah. You saw him?"

"He's hard to miss."

"Came in here with two horses to put up, said he needed some new ones. Asked me how much I wanted for Duke."

"And?"

"I told him he wasn't mine to sell," Adler said, "that he was yours."

"Mine?" Clint asked. "You mentioned my name?"

"Well, sure," Adler said. "Funny thing about

this Indian. Not only was he wearing a white man's gun, but he talked as good as a white man. Sure looked like an Indian, though."

"You told him I wasn't interested in selling?"

"I did."

"What did he say?"

"He said that anything was for sale at the right price," Adler said. "I got the impression he's used to getting what he wants."

"Well," Clint said, "not this time. If he comes back tell him I'm definitely not interested in selling, not at any price."

"I'll tell him."

"Better yet," Clint said, "tell him where I'm staying—the Liberty House—and tell him to come and see me. I'll tell him myself."

"However you want to do it," Adler said. "I ain't afraid of him, you know. I'm big enough to take care of myself."

"I know you are, Bill," Clint said, "but this comes under the heading of my business, doesn't it?"

"I guess so," Adler said. "Don't worry. I'll tell him what you said."

"Okay," Clint said. "What was the name of that café you mentioned?"

"The Golden Palace," Adler said. "You can't miss it. It's got a big front window with all sorts of golden designs on it. The lady's name is Mrs. Hollister, Kathy Hollister. Tell 'er I sent you over and that you're a friend of mine. She'll treat you right."

"I'll tell her," Clint said. "Thanks for your help."

Clint left the livery and started for the Golden Palace, thinking about the Indian who talked like a white man, wore a white man's gun, and was interested in good horses.

The description was starting to ring a bell in his mind.

Chapter Eight

Stan Barton sat in his room, staring into the blackness, which was all he could see. He'd been blind for three months, certainly not enough time to get used to it—and certainly not after thirty-eight years of seeing. All he could do now was reach inside his mind for the things he used to see and take for granted. The sun, the moon, the dirty streets of the towns where he was hired to uphold the law . . . and the faces of his wife and son. All gone now. No longer could he look at the sun and the moon, or the dirty ground. As for his wife and son . . . well, even if his sight somehow miraculously returned—which the doctors said was not beyond the realm of possibility—they wouldn't be around to see anymore.

They were dead.

Barton passed his hand over his face, rubbed it vigorously, then used his thumb and forefinger to massage his eyes. Rubbing his eyes did no good, though. When he took his hand away he was still blind.

Marshal Stan Barton. Blind.

How many men had he put away who would be happy to hear that? How many of them would be anxious to find him now? Even the cowards who refused to face him when he could see. Especially those bushwhackers!

And then there were the bastards who were responsible for it all, the death of his wife and son, and the loss of his eyesight. If they knew that he was tracking them, using John Running Deer as his eyes, what would they do? Would they run, or would they stop and wait for the blind man to catch up to them?

He hoped they would stop and wait. He sincerely hoped that word would get to them and they'd stop where they were and wait for him to catch up to them. All they had to do was stop and read a newspaper. He'd been interviewed a couple of times since the death of his family. He had told the newspapers that even without his eyesight he intended to track the killers down. With Running Deer at his side, he wasn't afraid to face them. They'd realize, just before they died, that they should have killed him when they had the chance. Instead, they had laughed, leaving him alive with the bodies of his wife and son pinning him down. He'd been too weak from his wounds to push them off—and even if he hadn't been wounded, grief had robbed him of any strength he might have had.

Now he cursed himself for being weak, for giving into the grief and letting the three killers get away. He should have been stronger then, but he'd be strong now. Blind or not, he'd find them and make them pay for what they had done.

Chapter Nine

Clint found the Golden Palace Café with no trouble. As Bill Adler had said, the big plate glass window was covered with gold swirls.

He entered and found the place only half full. It was close to dinnertime, and if the food was as good as Adler had said, why was it half empty? Then again, there were plenty of other eating establishments in town—and Adler did seem to have a special interest in this one.

"Are you alone?" a woman asked.

Clint studied her for a moment and wondered if this was the widow Hollister. She looked close to forty—could have gone either way—but she was a handsome woman with high cheekbones and a full mouth.

"Fella said I could get a good meal here."

"What fella would that be?" she asked.

"Bill Adler."

"Oh, Bill," she said. "He's always sending people over here."

"Did he send all of these?" Clint asked.

She looked around and laughed.

"No, I'm afraid you're the only one here who he sent today," she said. "I'm Kathy Hollister."

"Yes," Clint said, "he mentioned you."

"He did, eh?"

"Yes," Clint said, "he said some very nice things."

"Did you say you were eating alone?"

"I didn't say," Clint replied, "but yes, I am."

"Come and sit, then," she said.

He followed her to a small table against the wall. It afforded him a good view of the inside of the café, as well as the front door.

"What can I bring you?" she asked.

"Whatever your specialty is."

"And until it's ready?"

"Coffee," he said.

"How do you like it?"

"Hot and black."

"Coming up," she said.

As she walked away, Clint had the feeling that Adler had been a little fuzzy on the subject of who exactly was sweet on who.

Before leaving Stan Barton's hotel room John Running Deer had taken the man's key, so he was able to let himself in when he returned from the rooming house.

"That you, John?" Barton asked from the bed.

The curtain in the room was drawn, and the room was nearly dark. Of course, that didn't matter to Stan Barton, who was lying on his back on the bed.

"It's me, Marshal."

"Don't call me that," Barton said. "Did you get

yourself a place to stay?"

"Yes," Running Deer said, "a real nice place, as a matter of fact. Too bad we'll only be here for a day or two."

"Yeah," Barton said, sitting up, "too bad."

"Ready to go and eat?" Running Deer asked.

"I am kind of hungry," Barton said, reaching for his hat and finding it. He stood up, reached out for his gun belt, and put that on as well. "Did you find a place to eat?"

"The landlady at the rooming house recommended a place," Running Deer said. "Something called the Golden Palace."

"Doesn't have to be a palace," Barton said. "As long as the food is decent. Come on."

In the dark Barton found his way to the door. Running Deer opened it and they stepped out. The Indian put his hand on the white man's elbow, wondering if the man would protest, as he did half the time.

This time, he didn't.

Chapter Ten

Clint was eating his beef stew—not great, but certainly good—when the Indian and the white man entered the café. He noticed something odd right away. The Indian seemed to be guiding the white man, even though he was not always touching him. When he saw the man's eyes, Clint realized that he was blind. It was odd that a blind man would be wearing a gun.

He watched as Kathy Hollister showed them to a table and took their order. The white man sat with his hands in his lap, facing straight ahead.

The Indian's eyes were taking in the entire room. Clint watched, and as the Indian's eyes fell on him, settled, gauged him as a possible threat, and moved on, he suddenly recalled a newspaper article he had read recently about a blind ex-lawman who was searching for the men who had killed his family and cost him his sight. There was also something in the article about a sidekick who was an Indian. He couldn't recall any names at the moment, but it was too much of a coincidence for these men not to be the two in the newspaper.

Barton, that was the lawman's name. Sam? No . . . Stan, that was it, Stan Barton. He tried to drag the Indian's name from the same place he'd found the lawman's, but it was possible that the name had not even been mentioned in the article.

Clint was finishing up his meal when Kathy Hollister came out of the kitchen carrying the Indian's and Stan Barton's meals. The Indian was having steak and vegetables, while Barton looked to be dining simply on vegetables.

Clint ordered another pot of coffee from Kathy Hollister and tried to recall some more information that he might have read in the newspaper.

"I don't see why you don't let me order you a steak," John Running Deer said to Stan Barton.

"I've told you why, damn it," Barton said. "I won't sit here while people watch you cut my meat for me. Vegetables I can handle just fine all by myself."

As he said that a carrot slipped from his fork as he was lifting it to his mouth and fell into his lap. Running Deer held his breath, waiting to see if Barton would explode.

"Damn," Barton said, and brushed the fallen carrot from his lap, but he did not erupt. Instead he speared another one and put it in his mouth.

"You're getting better," Running Deer said. "There was a time when dropping a bit of food would have set you off."

"It still can," Barton said. "Sometimes I can control it, John, but sometimes I can't. It's just too damn hard sometimes."

Running Deer wanted to say he understood, but there was no way he could understand. He wasn't blind.

While they ate, Running Deer once again studied the other diners. There was a man seated against the wall opposite them who he guessed would pose the only threat—if indeed there was even a threat in the room. Ever since that time in Kansas when two diners suddenly leapt up and went for their guns, Running Deer saw everyone as a possible threat. They had been a couple of gun-crazy kids who saw a chance to take down an ex-lawman with a reputation, and it didn't bother them one bit that he was blind. Running Deer had upended their table, shoved Barton behind it, and then killed both men. Since that time he paid constant attention to the people in a room—whatever room they happened to be in at the time.

He noticed the man across from them studying them from time to time, and decided to ask the waitress a question when she came by again.

"Can I get you anything else?" Kathy Hollister asked them a few minutes later.

"A pot of coffee, after we've finished this fine meal," Barton said to her.

"Certainly."

"Excuse me," Running Deer said.

"Yes?"

"That man sitting across from us," he said, "he looks familiar. Do you know his name?"

She turned and looked over her shoulder, then back at Running Deer.

"No, I don't."

"He's a stranger in town, then?"

"Yes, he is," she said. "I believe he just arrived today, as a matter of fact—much the same as you and your friend."

"Thank you," Running Deer said.

As she moved away, Barton asked him, "What was that all about?"

"I think that's the man who owns the horse I want to buy."

"What makes you think that?"

"Because he's a stranger," Running Deer said.

"So are we."

"And how many more strangers do you think rode into town today?" Running Deer asked.

"John, sometimes I think you think too much," Barton said. "Why don't you go and ask him if he wants to sell his horse?"

"No," Running Deer said, "not here. Later."

"What if he doesn't want to sell it?" Barton asked.

Running Deer didn't answer.

"John?" Barton said. "I know you. You get stubborn about something and you don't let it go."

Running Deer still didn't answer.

"John," Barton said, his tone exhausted, "we don't have time for this kind of thing. We have a job to do, remember?"

"I remember," Running Deer said, "and to get it done we need good horses."

"We'll find horses," Barton said. "There's no need to get obsessed with one in particular."

"If you saw this one—" Running Deer started, and then he stopped, realizing what he was saying. "I'm sorry—" he started to apologize, but Barton cut him off.

"Never mind," he said, "it's fine. Don't worry about it. Just forget about the horse, all right? Just buy us a couple of new ones, the best ones you can find, and we'll make do."

Running Deer didn't reply. He was looking over at the man sitting against the other wall.

"John?"

"Don't worry, Stan," Running Deer said, "I'll get us a couple of horses."

Chapter Eleven

Clint looked over at the Indian and Stan Barton. The two men were deep in conversation about something, and every once in a while the Indian would look his way. This led him to believe that they were talking about him.

Kathy Hollister came over and asked him, "Can I get you anything else?"

"No," he said, "I'm full. That was a fine meal, Mrs. Hollister, just fine."

Actually, it was adequate, but he wanted to make her feel good.

"Well," she said, giving him a look that made him think about the size of Bill Adler, "if you feel that way, why don't you just have all your meals here?"

"Well," he said, standing up, "I might do that," although he had no intentions of having even one more meal here—not the way she was looking at him. Apparently she was not as sweet on Bill Adler as the man thought.

"Tell me something, Mrs. Hollister," he said, while he paid her for the meal.

"Sure," she said with a smile, "anything."

"Do you know those two men sitting over there?" He indicated Barton and the Indian with a slight jerk of his head.

She turned and looked over her shoulder at the Indian and the white man.

"No," she said, "they're strangers. I don't know anything about them except that the white man is blind and he wears a gun."

"I noticed that myself."

"Isn't that odd?"

"Yes," he said, "it is."

"And do you know something else?"

"What?"

"The Indian was asking me about you."

"Was he?"

"Yes."

"What did you tell him?"

"Nothing," she said, "I don't know anything about you—yet."

Her "yet" did not escape him, and he thought it was time he moved on. Kathy Hollister was attractive enough, but he did not want to get between her and Bill Adler.

"Well," he said, "thanks for the meal."

"Anytime," she said as he headed for the door. "Come back anytime."

As he went out the door, Clint thought he could feel the eyes of the two men on him, but then that was impossible. Barton was blind.

That meant it was just the eyes of the Indian he felt, boring into him.

Chapter Twelve

Rather than try the other saloon, Clint went back to the Broken Wheel. By now the gaming tables would be open. He didn't want to play any of the house games, though. He was hoping to find himself a private poker game.

When he walked in the door, the first person he saw was Bill Adler. It was hard not to notice the burly blacksmith, even though the place was now crowded with men drinking, talking, and gambling. He was standing at the bar with a mug of beer in his hand, and he was easily the biggest man in the place. As Clint approached the bar, Adler saw him and waved him over.

"There's my new friend," Adler said. It was clear from the way he was talking and gesticulating that he'd already had a few beers. "Come on over here, Clint, and I'll buy you a beer."

"I'll never turn down a free beer," Clint said.

There was barely room at the bar for Adler, but he used his elbows to make room for Clint to stand next to him. He nudged two men aside who, when they saw that the offending elbows belonged to Adler, obliged by squeezing over.

"Danny," Adler yelled to the bartender, "get my friend a beer."

"Comin' up," the bartender called.

Clint looked around the crowded room. He spotted the chubby brunette, Betty, who had tried to get him to go upstairs with her. He saw four other women working the room, the tall, thin blonde and three others. Two of them were also blond, and one was a redhead. Apparently, the owner believed in giving men equal choice. They were all young and attractive, but none had quite the physical bounty that the brunette had.

"How do you like Liberty so far, Clint?" Bill Adler asked.

"It seems like a nice town," Clint said, picking his beer up off the bar, "at least, what I've seen of it so far."

"Did you go over to the Golden Palace?"

"Uh, yes, I did."

Adler's eyes lit up and he asked, "What did you think of my Kathy?"

His Kathy?

"I thought the food was fine, Bill," Clint said. "Uh, thanks for the tip."

"No, no," Adler said, nudging Clint with a formidable elbow, "I meant what did you think of *her*?"

"Oh, her?" Clint asked. "Well . . . I thought she was . . . attractive . . . yes, very pretty."

"Yeah, she is pretty, ain't she?" Adler asked. His face was positively beaming as he talked about the woman. Clint hoped that, even if it was just in some small way, the woman returned his affection.

"Well, come on, drink up," Adler said, "we got lots of drinking to do tonight."

"Oh, not me," Clint said, shaking his head.

"Don't you like beer?"

"Sure, I like it," Clint said, "but not when I'm playing poker."

Adler looked confused.

"You ain't playin' poker."

"No," Clint said, looking around, "but I hope to be, fairly soon."

Danny, the bartender, leaned on the bar and said, "We don't have a house poker game."

Clint looked at him and said, "That's the best news I've heard since I got to town."

"Oh, you want a private game."

"That's right."

Danny looked around and said, "Well, judging from who I see here, one's liable to break out anytime now—that is, unless you want to get one started yourself."

"No, no," Clint said. "I'm a stranger here. I'll wait for a game to start and then see if there's an open chair for me."

"Well," Danny said, "as long as you're willing to wait."

"No problem," Clint said.

"Well, then," Adler said, "you can have another beer with me while you wait."

"Sure," Clint agreed, "just as soon as I finish this one."

While he was nursing that first beer Clint saw Betty, the brunette, start over toward him. As she approached him, she smiled widely. He found himself eyeing her impressive cleavage as she got closer.

"Well, hello," she said, sidling up to him, "you came back."

"I came back."

"But not for me, right?"

"Well, I—"

"I'm sorry," she said, laughing and putting her hand on his arm, "that wasn't fair, was it?"

"No," he agreed, laughing with her, "it sure wasn't."

"Well, nobody ever accused me of being fair," she said. "You intend to do some gambling?"

"I might."

Taking his arm in both hands now she said, "I could sort of hang on your arm—you know, bring you some good luck?"

"Is that your job?" Clint asked. "To bring customers good luck? I thought it was to distract them from what they were doing so they lose."

"Ooh," she said, removing her hands from his arm. "That was mean—but it's true," she added, with a giggle. "Somehow, though, I don't think you distract easy when you're gambling."

"I tend to concentrate when I have money at stake," Clint said.

"I guess I'd have to strip naked then to get you to notice me."

"You wouldn't have to strip naked for that, Betty," Clint said. "Me and the whole room notice you just the way you are."

"Oh," she said, eyeing him, "you *can* be nice, can't you?"

"I can be very nice" he said, then added, "under the right circumstances."

"Well," she said, turning her back but watching him over her shoulder, "I guess I'll just have to wait for the circumstances to be right."

As she sauntered away, swaying her fine butt suggestively, Bill Adler nudged Clint again and said, "Why don't you take her upstairs? I can tell she fancies you a lot."

"We've had that discussion," he said. "I don't generally pay to be with a woman."

"Why not?" Adler asked, looking confused.

Clint looked at him and said, "I like them to be with me by their own choice, Bill, not for money."

Adler frowned drunkenly and asked, "You get a lot of women that way?"

"I get my fair share," Clint said. "I'm going to check out some of the games, maybe watch for a while."

"I'll be right here, buddy," Adler said. "Come on back an' I'll buy you another drink."

Clint wondered if by the time he got back to the bar the big blacksmith would still be standing.

Chapter Thirteen

"Want a drink?" John Running Deer asked Stan Barton as they left the Golden Palace Café.

"Sure," Barton said. "I have a bottle in my room, though."

"No," Running Deer said, "I want a beer."

"Not me," Barton said.

"I'll take you back to the hotel," Running Deer said. "Then I'll go to the saloon."

"Suit yourself," Barton said indifferently.

His indifference changed, however, when they got outside his room.

"John, why don't you come inside and drink with me instead of going to the saloon?"

"What's the matter, Stan?" Running Deer asked. "Are you afraid I will get lost?"

"No, I—"

"Or that I'll get in trouble?"

"Yeah, that's it," Barton admitted. "I'm afraid you'll get yourself in trouble."

"I'm a grown man, Stan," Running Deer said. "If I want to get in trouble, I will."

"John—"

"But I don't want to get in trouble," Running Deer went on. "Don't worry about me, Stan. Just get some rest. Hey, maybe I'll even see about those horses."

"Yeah," Barton muttered as he entered his darkened room, "that's what I'm afraid of."

Inside Stan Barton groped his way to the bed and sat down wearily. He thought back over the past three months and realized that he wouldn't have gotten two feet without John Running Deer. Theirs was a strange friendship, one that seemed to deepen after Barton lost his sight.

He would never know for sure why Running Deer had agreed to ride with him and be his eyes throughout this manhunt. Certainly there was more to it then the money Barton was paying the man. The money was just a token amount, which the Indian had insisted on.

"It will keep our relationship on a business level," Running Deer had said, "in case anyone asks."

But there was more to it than that, Barton knew, much more.

What would he do, he wondered, if suddenly Running Deer decided to go his own way? How would he continue his hunt and get his revenge if that happened?

Chapter Fourteen

Running Deer found Clint Adams in the second saloon he looked in. He entered the Broken Wheel and stopped just inside the door. His size, and the fact that he was an Indian, immediately drew attention to him.

From his position next to the roulette wheel, where he was just watching the action and not playing, Clint saw Running Deer enter.

Running Deer ignored the attention he was getting and walked to the bar.

"We don't serve whiskey to Indians," Danny, the bartender, told him.

"I'll have a beer," Running Deer said.

"Can you pay?" Danny asked suspiciously.

"I can pay."

Running Deer saw that he was not going to get a beer until he showed the man his money, so he took a couple of coins out and put them on the bar.

"Beer," he said again.

"Comin' up," Danny said grudgingly. He scooped

the money off the bar top and went to draw the brew.

Running Deer continued to ignore the men around him while he sipped his beer, and gradually they stopped paying attention to him. Using the mirror behind the bar he located Clint Adams and kept his eyes on him.

Clint knew that the Indian was watching him, but he didn't know why. Did he know that Duke was his horse? Was that what this was about, or was it something else? Was the Indian looking to make a reputation for himself? That wasn't the impression he had gotten from reading the article on Stan Barton. Why would the Indian be traveling with Barton, helping him hunt for the men who had killed his family, if he was looking to build some kind of rep?

Over in a corner a poker game had started up about a half an hour before. Clint was waiting for the men to settle down before he approached, and he was satisfied to see that there was still an empty chair at the table. He'd wait a few more minutes before walking over.

Further down the bar from Running Deer the blacksmith, Bill Adler, was watching the Indian suspiciously. He saw that the Indian was watching Clint Adams, and he somehow felt responsible for this. If he had only told the Indian that the horse wasn't for sale without telling him who it belonged to, maybe the man wouldn't be watching Clint right now. Adler was determined that if trouble broke out he was going to help Clint Adams.

It was the least he could do for his new friend.

Clint watched the little white ball jump around on the wheel for the last time and walked away from the table without seeing what number it settled on. It was time to invite himself into the poker game.

Running Deer saw Clint Adams move away from the roulette table. He left his half-finished beer on the bar and moved to intercept him. He saw where Clint was headed—a poker game at a corner table—and he moved that way. Might as well get the business about the horse out of the way now.

"Clint Adams?" Running Deer said.

Clint stopped and stared at the Indian, who was now blocking his path.

"That's right."

"I want to talk to you."

"About what?"

"Your horse."

"What about him?"

"I want to buy him."

"He's not for sale," Clint told him firmly.

"Let's talk about a price."

"I said he's not for sale."

"At any price?"

"That's right," Clint said, "at any price. Now if you'll excuse me . . ."

He moved to go past the Indian, but the man grabbed him by the right arm. Because it was

his gun arm Clint pulled it away immediately,
to keep it free.

"Don't do that!" he snapped.

"I just want to talk to you about your horse,"
Running Deer said.

At that moment Bill Adler came up behind Running Deer and wrapped his arms around him.

"I got 'im, Clint!" he shouted.

"Bill, no!" Clint shouted.

Adler and the Indian were almost the same
size, but Adler was drunk and his balance was
gone. Running Deer forced his weight backward,
catching Adler off guard. Both men went crashing
to the floor, Running Deer twisting as they fell.
When they landed the Indian's right shoulder hit
the floor, and he felt a jolt of pain go from his
shoulder right down through his arm.

Adler lost his grip as they struck the floor, and
Running Deer rolled away, trying to ignore the
pain in his shoulder. He got to his feet before the
drunken Adler could, and the two men faced each
other.

Because of the similarity in size between the
two, men got up from their tables and moved
away, giving them room to fight. People started
to yell, and Clint could see that most of the men
were anticipating the fight, rooting for the blacksmith to smash the Indian. Clint, however, was
seeing things that they were not.

For one thing, Adler was too drunk to fight
and would probably end up getting hurt, or
worse.

In addition, the Indian had injured his shoulder
when he fell. Clint could see the pain etched on

the man's face, although the Indian was trying not to let it show.

"Come on, Bill, get 'im!" somebody shouted.

"Smash the redskin, Adler!" someone else called.

"Come on, Indian," Adler slurred drunkenly, swaying on his feet. "Come and get it."

The two men were about to clash when Clint drew his gun and fired.

Chapter Fifteen

"How bad is it?" Clint asked.

"Pretty bad," the doctor said. "He's not going to be able to use that arm for some time. He certainly won't be able to ride a horse for a while. The pain that would cause would be too great for anyone to bear—even someone with his apparent pain threshold. I don't know how he managed to get back to his feet after the injury."

"Stubborn, I guess."

"I guess," the doctor said. "What happened to Bill Adler?"

"Some of his friends took him to the livery to sleep it off," Clint told him.

"Somebody said you fired a shot," the doctor said.

"In the ceiling," Clint said, "to stop the fight from going any further."

"I see."

"Can I talk to him?"

"Sure," the doctor said. "See if you can convince him to stay put. He keeps insisting he has to go to the hotel to talk to some friend of his."

"I know," Clint said. "I'll talk to him."

Clint moved past the doctor and opened the door to the examining room. Inside was John Running Deer, whose shoulder had been seriously injured when he and Adler had fallen to the floor. The combined weight of the two big men had come down on that shoulder. Clint couldn't begin to imagine the pain that must have caused.

He also couldn't keep himself from feeling partially responsible for the whole incident. After all, Adler had thought he was helping him against the Indian.

As Clint entered, the Indian looked at him from the examining table. The doctor had bandaged the man around the chest and abdomen, pinning the injured arm inside the bandages.

"How do you feel?" Clint asked.

"Lousy."

Clint was at a loss for words for a moment, and then both men started to talk at one time.

"I only wanted to make an offer on your horse," the Indian said.

"I understand," Clint said, "but I'd already told you he wasn't for sale."

"What was your friend trying to do?"

"He was drunk," Clint said, "and he thought he was helping me. I'm sorry you got hurt. It was a misunderstanding."

"Yes," Running Deer said, "a misunderstanding."

They had exchanged names on the way to the doctor's office.

"Running Deer, I know about you and Stan Barton," Clint said.

"You do?"

"I read a newspaper account."

The Indian shook his head.

"I disagreed with that, but Stan insisted. He *wanted* the killers to know we were on their trail." He shook his head, remained silent a moment, then looked at Clint. "I have to go and talk to Stan. He's going to be very angry with me."

"For getting hurt?"

"He warned me about getting in trouble," Running Deer said. "I can't let this stop him from continuing on with his hunt."

"Do you think that's wise?"

Running Deer looked at Clint.

"I tried to talk him out of it from the beginning," he said, "but he's a stubborn man."

"Yes, but a blind man—"

"If you meet him," Running Deer said, "you'll find out that he's not just an ordinary blind man."

"Well," Clint said, "in any case, you're not going to be riding for a while."

"I'll ride," the Indian said.

"How?" Clint asked. "You can barely stand."

As if to try to prove Clint wrong, the Indian started to stand, but he staggered and would have fallen if not for Clint, who helped him back to a seated position on the table.

"Like I said," Clint repeated, "you can't ride."

"Now Stan will have to stay in town until I heal well enough to ride. His thirst for revenge is eating him up inside. I don't know how long he'll be able to sit still in this town."

"Well, he can't very well go looking for them without you, can he?"

"No," Running Deer said, shifting on the table, trying to get comfortable, "he can't."

"Are you staying at one of the hotels?" Clint asked.

"No," Running Deer said, "they wouldn't rent a room to an Indian."

"Where are you staying?"

"A rooming house at the end of town," Running Deer said, "but I have to talk to Stan."

"You've got to keep from moving around too much," Clint said. "I'll tell you what. Why don't I take you to your rooming house, and then I'll go and explain to Barton what happened."

"He'll still want to talk to me."

"Well, okay, then I'll walk him over to the rooming house to see—uh, to talk to you."

Running Deer thought it over for a moment, then nodded and said, "All right."

"After all," Clint added, saying it aloud for the first time, "I feel to blame for this, in a way."

Later, he'd feel sorry that he *had* said it out loud.

Chapter Sixteen

Clint walked John Running Deer over to the rooming house, where he left him in the capable hands of his very attractive landlady, Molly Mulligan.

"I hope you don't expect me to nurse you until you're well," she was saying as she assisted him into the house. Clint had the feeling that was exactly what she was going to end up doing.

From the rooming house he walked over to the hotel to talk to Stan Barton.

Before leaving the doctor's office with John Running Deer, though, they had both had to talk to the sheriff, a man named Roe Healy. Sheriff Healy seemed to be a no-nonsense type who didn't like strangers stirring up trouble in his town. He wanted to know who started the trouble and who fired the shot. Clint took the time to explain that the whole thing had been the result of a misunderstanding, and that no one was going to press charges.

"What about the hole in the ceiling of the saloon?" Healy asked.

"Is it the only hole there?" Clint asked.

"That ain't the point," the sheriff said.

"I'll pay for the hole in the ceiling," Clint said finally, and the sheriff left it at that.

Now Clint entered the Doubletree Hotel and asked the desk clerk what room Stan Barton was in.

"You better watch out, though," the clerk said after giving him the number, "that Indian might be around somewhere."

"He's dangerous, huh?" Clint asked.

"Ain't they all?"

Clint ignored the man after that and went upstairs. He found the room he was looking for and knocked on the door.

"Who is it?"

"A friend," Clint said. Then he added, "My name's Clint Adams. I have a . . . a message from John Running Deer."

There was silence from the other side of the door, and then the voice asked, "Where is John? Why isn't he here himself?"

"He's at his rooming house," Clint said. "There was an accident—this would be easier if I could come inside."

"I'm going to unlock the door," the voice said, "but don't come in until I say so."

"All right."

He heard the key turn in the lock, then several seconds went by while he heard movement from inside the room.

"All right," the voice called, "come on in."

Clint opened the door and stepped inside. The curtain in the room was drawn, and since darkness had fallen outside, the room was black.

"Hello?"

"Just stand fast and tell me what's on your mind," Barton said. "I have a gun on you."

Clint realized that in the dark a blind man had the advantage over a sighted man—but he didn't want to play that game. Besides, given enough time his eyes would adjust to the dark. Barton's never would.

"Barton, listen," Clint said, "there was an accident today and Running Deer was hurt."

"How bad?"

"His shoulder—"

"Was he shot?"

"No," Clint said. "He fell on his shoulder during a fight."

"How bad is he hurt?" Barton asked again.

"Bad enough to keep him off a horse for a while."

"Goddamn it!" Barton swore. "What did you have to do with it?"

"This is very awkward—"

"Never mind," Barton said. "I like the dark."

Clint's eyes were starting to adjust. He could make out the silhouette of a man standing by the bed.

"You'd make a smaller target if you'd crouch," Clint said to him.

"Wha—"

"My eyes are adjusting to the dark, Barton," Clint said. "If I wanted you dead, you would be by now. Put the gun away and let me light a lamp so we can talk."

There was a moment's hesitation and then Barton asked, "Do you know . . . ?"

"About your blindness?" Clint asked. "Yes, I do. Running Deer told me."

"Running Deer has a big mouth these days," Barton said.

"It doesn't matter," Clint said. "I also saw both of you at the café earlier. You hide it well for the most part, but I was able to notice."

"What's your name again? I didn't hear you the first time."

"Clint Adams."

"Adams?" Barton repeated. "The Gunsmith?"

"That's right."

Clint heard the sound of the hammer of the gun being eased down.

"All right," Barton said, "I guess you're right. If you wanted me dead, I couldn't stop you. Go ahead, light a lamp and tell me what that bull-headed Indian's got himself into this time."

Chapter Seventeen

Clint turned up the lamp on the wall just enough so that he could see Barton seated on the bed. The ex-lawman had uncocked his gun, but it was still on the bed right near his hand, where he could get at it. His eyes stared sightlessly ahead, and Clint realized that he was being silly by not turning the lamp up all the way. Still, he left the room dim.

Briefly, he explained to Barton what had happened in the saloon.

"That was your horse he was talking about, huh?" Barton said when Clint finished.

"I guess so."

"I told him to forget about it, but he wouldn't listen," the blind man said. "I guess that must be some horse, huh?"

"He's impressive, yes."

"Well," Barton said, standing up, "I guess I'd better go and see the dumb redskin."

"He said you'd be mad at him."

"For what?" Barton asked. He took his gun belt from the bedpost and strapped it on, then picked the gun up off the bed and put it in the holster. "For getting hurt?"

"He said you'd be mad that you'd have to wait for him to heal before you start your hunt again."

"Well," Barton said with a frown, "I'm disappointed, sure, but no, I'm not mad at him."

He started to reach for something, and Clint realized he was looking for his hat. He saw it on the floor across the room. The man must have kicked it when he got off the bed to unlock the door.

"If you're looking for your hat, it's over here," Clint said, retrieving it.

"Oh, thank you," Barton said. He put his hand out and Clint placed the hat in it. "I'm always kicking the damned thing."

"Would you like me to walk you over to the rooming house?" Clint asked.

"I guess you'd better," Barton said. "Ain't much chance of me finding it otherwise."

"I guess not," Clint said.

He opened the door, then turned to watch Barton coming across the room toward him. The man obviously knew where the bed was, because he avoided it nicely. He put his hand on the open door and then walked out into the hall. Clint closed the door and stood in the hall next to him.

"Uh . . . how can I help you?" he asked, feeling awkward.

"Just let me hold you by the arm with my left hand," Barton said.

"My right arm?" Clint asked.

"Oh, you're probably right-handed," Barton said. "That's your gun arm, right?"

"Yes, but—"

"No, no," Barton said, "move to my other side and I'll hold your left elbow. I usually keep my gun hand free—old habits die hard—but it makes more sense for your hand to be free than mine."

Clint moved to Barton's right side, and the man took hold of his left arm.

"If we had done this before, you'd just have to hold my elbow and steer me," Barton said. "All you've really got to do is warn me about stairs and steps and such."

"I can do that," Clint said, but he was nervous. In fact, he was extremely nervous on the stairs until they made it to the lobby without incident.

"Well, we did okay on the stairs," Barton said, "the rest of the way should be easy, right?"

"I suppose . . ." Clint said, but he wasn't at all sure.

Molly Mulligan walked John Running Deer up to his room and helped him get into bed.

"Get undressed," she said.

He looked at her.

"Down to your underwear, if you like," she said. "I've seen men in their underwear before."

"I am a Blackfoot," he said. "I don't wear any underwear."

"Oh," she said, but she was only thrown for a couple of seconds. "Well, I've seen naked men, too. Get undressed and into bed."

He hesitated, then started to pull off his buckskin trousers with one hand.

"Oh, let me help," she said. "Sit down."

He had gotten the pants down to his thighs, and now he sat so that she could pull them off. He extended his legs, aware that his penis was beginning to thicken. On her knees she pulled the trousers off and suddenly she saw his semierect penis.

"Oh . . . my . . ." she said. She licked her lips, which at that particular point in time he found to be a very sexy thing for her to do—and suddenly his penis was rigid.

She stared at the large column of flesh and then looked at his face. He stared back at her, making a conscious effort not to look sheepish or embarrassed.

She, too, was attempting not to appear non-plussed by the situation, so it came down to the two of them trying to appear calm—calmer than the other.

Or, she thought, perhaps more in control was the right phrase. Who was more in control of this situation? she wondered.

Well, there was one way to make sure that *she* was in control.

Slowly, she ran her left hand up his right leg, enjoying the firm muscle of his calf, then his thigh. She could smell the scent emanating from his crotch. She had smelled men before, but never an Indian. It smelled different . . . and good.

She ran her other hand up his other leg, and then both of her hands were on his naked thighs. He was sitting, leaning his weight back on his good arm, and watching her in fascination. Was she really going to . . .

And then she touched him, very gently with her index finger and middle finger. She ran them up the length of him, feeling the smoothness of the underside of his penis. She moved up on to her knees, getting her face closer, breathing in the scent of him more deeply.

His penis began to redden as she closed her hand around it and gently stroked it up and down. Her eyes watched as the mushroomlike head swelled and turned almost purple.

No one, she remembered thinking, is in control of *this* situation. *This* was totally out of control.

"Um," she said, and he watched in fascination as she opened her mouth, ducked her head, and took him all the way inside. . . .

Chapter Eighteen

Their progress walking from the hotel to the rooming house was slow, and a couple of times Barton stumbled because Clint forgot to tell him to be careful with a step up or down. Each time Clint apologized, and each time Barton told him it was all right.

As they walked, they talked, and Barton told Clint about the death of his wife and child.

"I didn't see it coming, God help me," Barton said. "Apparently they rode out to my house to gun me down before they went to town to rob the bank. I came out of the house with my wife and my son ahead of me, and they opened fire. They were just sitting there on their horses, and as soon as the door opened they started shooting. If I'd gone out the door first . . ."

"You'd be dead right now, in addition to your family," Clint said. "And then who would there be to hunt these men down?"

"Sure," Barton said, shaking his head, "so a blind man will hunt them down."

"Apparently you believe that, or else why would you be here?"

"I believe it," Barton said, "most of the time. Sometimes, though . . ."

"It's natural to have doubts," Clint said. "Everybody does."

They walked along in silence for a few moments and then Barton said, "You think I'm crazy, don't you?"

"No," Clint said immediately.

"A blind man hunting three sighted men? Why the hell not?"

"Because I've been on enough manhunts of my own," Clint said, "some personal and some not. Nobody can understand what's driving you but you, Barton, but if I can't understand, I'm certainly not going to judge you for it."

Barton hesitated, then said, "You do understand, don't you?"

"Maybe," Clint said, "maybe I do. . . ."

Molly Mulligan's head was bobbing up and down between John Running Deer's legs, but he couldn't see her. He had long since dropped down onto his back, and it hurt his shoulder too much to try to look down at her from that position. Instead, he reached for her with his free hand and put it on her head, so he felt her head bobbing up and down, and he certainly felt her hot, avid mouth sliding wetly up and down the length of his penis.

She had released him from her mouth once, but that was only to run her anxious mouth over his thighs, then up over his belly. Even while she was doing that, though, her hands were on him, stroking him, pulling on him, teasing him, fondling his testicles, and then she was on him again with her mouth, taking him inside, obviously intent on milking him dry.

Suddenly, he felt the wave crashing up from his ankles, through his legs, and out his penis, filling her mouth.

"Mmmm," she said, but she didn't let him loose. She sucked on him until he was drained, and then and only then did she let his penis slide free of her mouth.

She stood up then and looked down at him.

"Slide around," she said, moving him up on the bed until his head was on the pillow.

She pulled the sheet up over him, covering his nakedness and his now limp penis, but not without giving it one last look. She was amazed by what had happened, but it had been thrilling, also. However, she was trying to hide both emotions from him.

"There," she said, putting her hand on his bare, hairless chest, "that should relax you for a while."

She was surprised when Running Deer growled and reached for her with his good hand. He caught her by the arm and pulled her down to him so that he could kiss her, deeply, wetly, thrusting his tongue into her mouth. When he let her go she was breathless, staring at him, her eyes wide. She didn't know Indians kissed, let alone like *that*.

"Next time," he said gruffly, "you get undressed, too."

She was about to answer when she heard someone pounding on the door downstairs.

"I—I have to get that. . . ." she said, backing

toward the door of his room. When she reached it she went outside, starting to close the door behind her, but suddenly she stopped and stuck her head back into the room.

"If there is a next time," she told him with a smile and closed the door.

John Running Deer caught his breath for the first time in minutes and ran his good hand over his face and chest. He could hardly believe what had happened, but it *had* happened, and the white woman had better believe that there would be a next time.

And then John Running Deer frowned as he realized for the first time that his shoulder was killing him.

Chapter Nineteen

By the time Molly Mulligan opened the front door she thought she had regained her composure. To Clint Adams, though, she looked like a woman who was out of breath from some sort of exertion. Housework, he wondered, or something else?

She recognized Clint immediately. After all, he'd been there less than an hour ago with John Running Deer.

"Bringing me another charity case?" she asked.

"No," Stan Barton said, "no charity case, ma'am. I'm John Running Deer's friend. I'd like to see him, please?"

"Hey," she said, looking him in the eye, "oh God, you're, uh . . ."

"That's right, ma'am," he said, "I'm blind. Can I, uh, talk to him?"

"Oh, gee, mister, I'm sorry—"

"It's all right," Barton said. "Really. I'd just like to talk to my friend."

"Uh, sure," she said, "come on, follow me—I mean, I'll show you—I mean—"

"Just lead on, Miss Mulligan," Clint said. "We'll follow along."

"Uh, okay. . . ."

She showed them up to John Running Deer's door and said, "That's it. He might be asleep by now, though. He was pretty, uh, tired when I left him."

Clint studied her closely, and when she noticed this, she blushed. She couldn't help it.

"Yes," Clint said with a smile, "I bet he was."

"I, uh, have work to do," she said, and fled back downstairs.

"What was that all about?"

"She was out of breath," Clint said, "sweaty, and a little . . . excited."

Barton frowned and said, "I thought you said he was hurt."

"He is."

"Jesus," Barton said, "he likes white women, and they like him."

"Interesting."

Barton knocked on the door loudly, and Running Deer called out, "Come in."

"Want me to wait downstairs?" Clint asked.

"Hell, no," Barton said, "we ain't gonna say anything you can't hear."

He opened the door, and they both went in.

Downstairs Molly Mulligan went to her own room and sat on her bed, her hands clasped in her lap. She was still breathing hard, still tasting the Indian in her mouth. An Indian! If anyone had ever told her she'd do . . . *that* to an Indian . . . but it had almost been like she had no choice.

After all, it had been she who told him to undress, and then she offered to help him. Had she known that would happen? Did she want it to happen? Did she want it to happen again?

Oh, yes. . . .

"You red-skinned son of a bitch," Barton said as they entered the room.

"I knew you'd be mad," John Running Deer said from the bed.

"I'm not mad," Stan Barton said. "You had her, didn't you?"

"Had who?"

"Had who," Barton said. "The white woman, your landlady. I don't know what white women see in you, Running Deer, but you did it again, didn't you?"

"More like she did it," Running Deer said. "She practically raped me. . . ."

"Oh, sure."

"She did," Running Deer said, and then lowered his voice and added, "with her mouth."

"Look at his face," Barton said to Clint.

"I'm looking at it."

Up till now Clint had only seen the Indian's face as impassive. Here he was seeing more expression than he'd seen before.

"Is his mouth open?"

"Wide open."

"Son of a bitch," Barton said. "He's not lying."

Barton moved across the room until his knees struck the bed. He groped for the sheet, grabbed it, and pulled it off Running Deer.

"Is he naked?"

"As the day he was born," Clint said.

"Son of a bitch," Barton said. "He's telling the truth."

"Of course I'm telling the truth," Running Deer said. "When have I ever lied to you, Stan?"

"Today."

"Today?" Running Deer said. "When?"

"When you told me you weren't looking for trouble. Remember that?"

"I wasn't."

"But you found it, didn't you?"

"More like it found me."

"So you end up here," Barton said, "with an Indian-hungry landlady."

"I'll be up and out of here in a couple of days," Running Deer said.

"I don't think so."

"Well . . . not much longer than that."

"Oh, a lot longer, I think."

Running Deer stared at the blind man, and then Clint saw another expression cross his face—one of genuine sadness.

"I'm sorry, Stan," Running Deer said. "I really am."

"Don't worry about it," Barton said. "Just heal up, all right?"

"I will," Running Deer said. "But what about you? I know we had a hot trail to follow—"

"I'll still following it."

"How?"

"With your replacement."

"What replacement?" John Running Deer asked, looking puzzled. "You found a replacement for me already?"

"Just a temporary one," Barton said. "Don't worry, I'll keep in touch so you always know where we are, and when you're able to ride you can catch up."

"Who's the replacement?"

"Don't worry about that, John," Barton said, moving away from the bed. "You just get yourself well, and enjoy your landlady."

Barton turned to Clint and said, "Do me a favor, will you?"

"What?"

"Cover him up," Barton said. "There's nothing more disgusting than a naked Indian."

Barton felt for the door and went out into the hall. Clint hurriedly picked up the sheet and tossed it back over the Indian, then followed Barton.

"Where to?" Clint asked.

"I think I'd like a drink," Barton said. "Let's go to a saloon."

"Okay," Clint said.

They didn't run into the landlady on the way down, so they let themselves out.

"Pick out a small saloon, will you?" Barton said. "Not the same one you and John messed up tonight."

"We'll try the Red Saddle."

Barton took Clint's elbow, and they started back toward the center of town.

"By the way," Clint said, "Why did you lie to him about a replacement?"

"I didn't."

"Sure you did," Clint said. "I've been with you

for the past hour. You didn't have time to get a replacement for him."

"Sure I did," Barton said.

"No," Clint said, "I'm the only one you've seen . . . hey, wait a minute!"

Clint stopped walking, but Stan Barton continued on as if he could see and said, "Let's talk about it over a drink."

Chapter Twenty

The Red Saddle was much smaller than the Broken Wheel, with no gaming tables, and only a few girls working. In fact, there were very few customers. Clint walked Stan Barton to a back table, then went to the bar to get two beers from the bored-looking bartender. He took them back to the table and sat across from Barton. The ex-lawman took the mug in his left hand, took a drink, and then set it down on the table, keeping his hand on it.

"When did you get this idea about me replacing Running Deer?" Clint asked.

"When I said it," Barton replied. "I hadn't thought of it before, but it makes sense."

"This I've got to hear," Clint said. "How does it make sense?"

Barton paused to sip his beer before answering.

"It's your fault."

"What's my fault?"

"That John got hurt."

Clint sat back and shook his head.

"Come on," Barton said, as if he could see Clint's head shaking, "you've thought that, too, haven't you?"

"Well," Clint said slowly, "I *have* given it some thought that I should take *partial* responsibility for what happened."

"You see?" Barton said. "Then it makes perfect sense that you replace John as my eyes for as long as it takes for him to recover."

"For as long as it takes—"

"Well," Barton reasoned, "it won't take that long, will it? I mean, it's not like you're being sentenced to five years of service."

"No, but . . . I'm actually a little flattered that you'd want me, Barton—"

"Call me Stan," Barton said. "If we're going to be riding together you can call me Stan, and I'll call you Clint."

"Well," Clint said, "we can be on a first-name basis, Stan, I have no problem with that, but I haven't agreed to ride with you—"

Suddenly Stan Barton's hand darted out and grabbed Clint's arm, where it was resting on the table. Clint was startled. It was as if the blind man could see it.

"Clint," Barton said, "I need you. I had a fair chance of catching up to them with John Running Deer, and then getting killed, but with you I have the same chance of catching them, and a better chance of coming out of it alive."

"Wait a minute, Stan," Clint said, "this is beginning to sound uncomfortably like you think you're hiring my gun. I don't hire my gun out."

"I'm not hiring your gun," Stan Barton said.

"I'm asking you for your help because I know you understand this. You understand what I'm doing, and why I have to do it."

That much was true. He did understand what was going on inside the man that would drive him this way—and it *was* partially his fault that Running Deer had gotten hurt.

"What do you say, Clint?" Barton squeezed his arm, and then released it.

"When would you want to leave?"

"Well, I need a new horse," Barton said. "We could do that tomorrow."

"Are we following a trail that will grow a day colder if we wait?"

"No," Barton said. "We had some information about a gang that was operating in Colorado. That's where we were headed."

"So we could get your horse tomorrow, outfit ourselves, and leave in the morning?"

"Right."

"Colorado?"

"Right."

They could be in Colorado in three days' time. Of course, if he agreed to this, then he was not only agreeing to help Barton find the men who killed his family, but also to bring them in or— as Barton was probably thinking—to kill them.

"I'm not going to help you just kill three men, Stan," Clint said. "If that's what you have in mind, forget it."

"If we can bring them back, then that's what we'll do," Barton said. "I'll be just as satisfied to see them swing from a rope."

Clint frowned, but then he knew what Barton

meant. He couldn't actually *see* them swing. . . .

"Of course," Barton said, "there's always the chance that they'll resist. . . ."

"I think we'll just deal with that when the time comes," Clint said.

"Good," Barton said. "Then that means you'll do it? You'll help me?"

"Against my better judgment," Clint said, "and only because you've made me feel guilty about Running Deer's injury . . . yes, I'll help you."

"Good," Stan Barton said, a look of relief coming over his face. "Then let's drink to our partnership."

"Our *temporary* partnership," Clint amended.

"Yes," Barton said, "of course."

Chapter Twenty-One

They finished their beers, and then Clint walked Stan Barton back to his hotel room. Barton told Clint there'd be no need to check on him again that night, that he would stay inside until morning.

"I trust you to get me a good horse," Barton said. "Of course, I'll pay for it. Do you want some money now? For the horse and supplies?"

"No," Clint said, "I'll tell you when I need money, and how much. I'll come and get you early in the morning, about seven?"

"Six, seven, it doesn't matter," Barton said. "I don't sleep much since . . . since I lost my eyesight."

Clint thought he was going to say something else, like maybe that he didn't sleep much since his wife and son had been killed. Maybe when he slept, he dreamed about it. That would be enough to keep any man awake.

Clint left the hotel and went over to the livery stable. He knew that Bill Adler would be there, and that there was a chance he'd be asleep. By waking him up and dealing with him now—

making the man feel guilty—maybe he'd be able to get a good price on a horse.

The front doors of the livery were open, and Clint went inside. It was dark, but he found a lamp hanging on the wall near the door and lit it. He turned it up and first found his way to Duke's stall. The big gelding stood calmly and eyed him.

"No, we're not leaving yet," Clint said. "Just came to see how you were doing."

Clint realized that when he was finished with helping Stan Barton, he was going to have to come back here to pick up his rig and team. Well, that couldn't be helped. He'd already agreed to be Barton's "eyes"—the first time he'd ever done anything like *that*—and he'd just have to make the trip back here when they were done—or when John Running Deer had recovered enough to catch up to them.

He rubbed the big gelding's nose and looked around for Bill Adler. He became aware of heavy, even breathing. He followed the sound and discovered Adler lying in some hay where he had apparently been dumped.

"Hey, Bill!" Clint called.

The man didn't move.

"Come on, Bill," Clint said, putting his foot on the man and nudging him.

When the man still didn't move, Clint sort of kicked him in the side with his toe—not too hard, but enough to wake him.

"Wha—who—" Adler said, coming awake and looking around bleary-eyed.

"It's me, Clint Adams."

"Oh," Adler said, rubbing his face. He dropped his hands and looked around. "What happened? How did I get here?"

"You were carried," Clint said. "After the fight you passed out."

"Fight?" Adler said. "What fight?"

Amazingly the man seemed sober—disoriented, but sober.

"You don't remember the fight?" Clint asked. "Well, actually it wasn't much of a fight."

"You and me had a fight?"

"No," Clint said, "not you and me, you and a big Indian named John Running Deer."

"Oh," Adler said. "Who won?"

"Nobody," Clint said. "I stopped it before it could go too far."

"How did you stop it?"

Clint stared at him.

"You really don't remember any of this, Bill?" he asked.

"Um, no," Adler said. He staggered to his feet and said, "I need a drink of water."

While Adler had his water, Clint explained to the man what had happened in the saloon.

"So you didn't need any help?"

"No, I didn't."

"Well," Adler said, "I don't think very straight when I'm drunk."

"How come you're not still drunk?" Clint asked. "I mean, only a little while ago you were real drunk, and now . . ."

"Oh, I'm like that," Adler said. "I just need a little bit of sleep and it clears my head. Gee, I'm sorry that Indian got hurt, but he's lucky I was drunk, or he might have gotten hurt worse."

Clint wasn't quite sure who would have gotten "hurt worse" if both men had been on even terms, but he didn't mention that.

"I need to buy a horse, Bill."

"What? What's wrong with your horse?"

"Nothing," Clint said, "but because you hurt John Running Deer, I agreed to ride with Stan Barton until the Indian healed up, and Barton needs a horse."

"This is the blind guy, right?"

"Right."

"And you have to go with him because I hurt the Indian?"

"That's right."

Suddenly Bill Adler smiled.

"What's so funny?"

"Now I know why you're disappointed that I ain't drunk," Adler said, "and I sure ain't stupid."

"What do you mean?"

"You're trying to make me feel guilty so I'll give you a good price on a horse."

Clint looked stung by the accusation.

"Would I do that?"

"Yeah," Adler said, putting one huge hand on Clint's shoulder, "but that's okay, I *will* give you a good price. Let's go outside and you can pick one out."

Chapter Twenty-Two

Clint purchased a handsome gray colt from Bill Adler, convinced that he had gotten the best price possible for Stan Barton. He told Adler to have both horses saddled in the morning and ready to go.

"What about your rig?"

"I'll have to leave it here until I finish and can come back for it."

"Okay," Adler said, "I'm sure we can come to a fair price."

"For what?"

"Space rental. . . ."

Clint left the livery after making a deal with Adler to keep his rig and team until he came back. He went from there to the general store and caught the owner just before he closed. He bought enough supplies for a few days, figuring that once they crossed into Colorado they could stop again for more.

After that he went back to the Broken Wheel to see if that poker game was still going on. He never did get a chance to sit in.

When he entered the saloon, he went to the bar first for a beer. The bartender, Danny, was looking at him strangely as he served him.

"You ain't gonna put any more holes in the ceiling, are you?" he asked finally.

"I don't think so," Clint said, picking up his beer. "Think I'll have a reason?"

"I didn't think you had a reason before," Danny said. "A lot of us wanted to see who'd win that fight."

"Well, sorry I spoiled your fun," Clint said.

He turned his back to the bar and looked over at the table where the poker game had been going on, but it was empty. Apparently the game hadn't lasted very long.

The gaming tables were still in action, though, and the place itself was still packed. In fact, it looked even more crowded than it had before—suddenly *too* crowded.

"Too many people here, huh?" Betty asked as she moved up next to him.

"I was just thinking the same thing," he said. "Maybe I'll finish this beer and head somewhere else."

"I don't blame you," she said. "I wish I could leave early."

Clint drank some of his beer, then decided to leave the rest. He put the mug down on the bar and looked at Betty.

"I'll be leaving in the morning, Betty," he said. "I'm sorry we couldn't . . . get together."

"In the morning?" she said, obviously disappointed. "So soon?"

"Sooner than I thought, too," he said, shaking his head.

"Listen," she said impulsively, "I get finished here at three."

He stared at her and said, "Uh-huh?"

"Would that be too late?"

"For what?"

"For me to come to your room, silly."

"I thought we talked about this—"

"For free."

"Free?"

"Yes," she said, "free."

"Now why would you want to go and do that?" he asked, teasing her.

"Because I'm curious," she said, "and this is my only chance to satisfy my curiosity."

He decided not to tell her that he'd be coming back—not yet, anyway.

"Well, if you're not too tired," he said, "I sure won't be."

"Leave your door unlocked."

She said this low, leaning closer to him so no one would hear.

"I can't do that," he said.

With his reputation, he was not in the habit of leaving his doors unlocked.

"Just knock," he told her, "and I'll hear you."

"You'd better," she said, "or I'll wake the whole hotel."

"Don't worry," he said, "I'll hear you."

"Okay," she said, looking excited. "I'll be there. See you later."

"I'm looking forward to it."

She touched his arm lightly and moved away

to do her job. Clint watched her until she melted into the crowded room, then he turned and left.

He was very much looking forward to having her come to his room.

Chapter Twenty-Three

"Remember what you said this afternoon?" Molly asked John Running Deer.

The Indian opened his eyes and saw her standing there by the bed.

"What?"

"About my clothes," she said.

"What did I say?" he asked.

"This," she said, and he watched as she removed all of her clothing. She stood there naked then, long and lean, small breasts, firm nipples, pink and erect, almost no hips at all on her. Her skin, though, was smooth and firm, and she smelled like she was fresh from a bath—which she was.

"Oh," he said.

She got on the bed with him and pulled the sheet down away from him. He was still naked, which was the way he always slept anyway. All he was wearing was that bandage that pinned his left arm to his side.

"You just relax, John," she said into his ear. "Let Molly do it all."

She kissed him then, first his mouth, then his neck, then his shoulder, and on from there, over his chest, pausing to tongue his nipples. . . .

"Today was the first time I ever tasted an Indian," she said, with her mouth on his belly.

"W-what did you think?" he asked. His heart was pounding, and his penis was throbbing.

"Ooh, I liked it," she said, moving down even further until she was comfortably nestled between his spread legs. "You're very big, you know," she said, running her fingers up the underside of his erection.

"Yes, I know. . . ."

"And pretty," she said, "so pretty."

She kissed the head of his penis, a big, juicy kiss, and then ran her tongue down the length of him. For a moment he thought she was going to take him into her mouth, as she had done earlier, but instead she straddled him.

"I'll be gentle," she said, "I promise. . . ."

Suddenly, he was inside of her. She just lifted her hips, held him with her hand, and settled down on him, taking him inside of her.

"Ooh, God . . ." she groaned as she started to move up and down on him. "Oh, Christ, yes. . . ."

He couldn't just lie there any longer. After all, he did have one free arm. He reached up and palmed one of her small breasts, rubbed the nipple with his thumb, and then did the same to the other one. Her eyes were closed, her head was thrown back, and beads of sweat began to run down between her breasts and beyond as she rode him slowly, gently, but steadily.

"Ooh . . . ooh . . . ooh . . ." she said, one "ooh" for every time she came down on him.

He slid his hands between her breasts, getting her sweat on his fingers, and then moved down over her belly until he reached the point where they were joined. With his thumb he probed into her pubic hair, found her clit, and began to stroke it.

Her eyes widened, and she looked down at him.

"Jesus," she said, and suddenly she forgot about being gentle as waves of pleasure rolled over her. . . .

"I'm sorry," she said, moments later, out of breath. "I didn't mean to hurt you."

He was about to tell her that it didn't hurt at all—a lie—when they became aware of someone knocking on the door downstairs.

She stretched out next to him and licked his shoulder. She still hadn't gotten enough of the "taste" of the Indian.

"Aren't you going to answer the door?" he asked.

"Someone else will," she said. "I'm too tired to go downstairs."

She pressed the length of her slender body against his, and he slid his good arm around her so that she could snuggle even closer. Her flesh was hot and damp from perspiration. He'd never been with a woman—white or Indian—who sweat so much during sex. What would it be like, he thought, to have sex with her in the summer?

He caught himself then. Why was he thinking like that? He'd be gone well before the summer came. It was three months away, and his injury would not keep him here that long.

He looked down at her head on his chest and saw that she was having trouble keeping her eyes open. He hoped she wouldn't sleep *too* long, because he hadn't had his fill of the "taste" of an Irish white woman.

They heard someone pounding down the steps to answer the door—the man was cursing and muttering as he went past their door—and then Running Deer suddenly realized that it might be Stan Barton coming back to see him.

"Molly . . ."

"Hmm?"

"Molly," he said, shaking her, "you'd better get dressed."

"Wha—" she started to say, but at that point there was a knock on his door.

Chapter Twenty-Four

Clint knocked on the door of the rooming house until it was opened by an irate-looking man in his fifties. He wondered why the landlady, Molly Mulligan, wasn't answering instead of this man who he had obviously awakened.

"What?" the man snapped.

"Sorry," Clint said, "but there's somebody here I have to talk to."

"Well, go ahead and talk," the man said. "I got to get back to sleep."

The man disappeared and left the door open. Clint entered, closed the door behind him, and retraced the steps from that afternoon that had taken him to John Running Deer's room. The door was closed, and he knocked gently. He realized now that he couldn't possibly have gotten into the rooming house without waking somebody up, but he felt it was necessary to tell John Running Deer that he and Barton would be leaving the next day.

He knocked again and suddenly the door was opened. He was surprised—or was he—to see

92

Molly Mulligan standing there. She was dressed, but her hair was a mess and her face was flushed.

"Oh, sorry," he said, "I just wanted to talk to John Running Deer."

"It's late," she said.

"I know," he said. "I'm sorry, but we're leaving in the morning. I thought he should know."

"What's your name?"

"Clint Adams."

"John," she said, over her shoulder, "Clint Adams is here."

"Let him in."

She moved aside and let him enter, then she turned and said to the man on the bed, "I'll check in on you later."

She left the room, closing the door behind her. If there was any question as to what he had interrupted, the smell in the room dispelled it. He knew what that smell was, because he had smelled it many times before in rooms where he had had sex with a woman. There was something about a man and a woman's bodies together that produced a very distinctive scent.

"Bad timing," Clint said to the Indian. "I'm sorry."

"Forget it," Running Deer said, "she'll be back. What can I do for you?"

"I thought you should know that Barton and I will be leaving in the morning."

"You're the replacement, huh?"

Clint shrugged.

"Temporarily, until you're back on your feet," he said. "It's the least I can do."

"He made you feel guilty, right?"

Clint grinned and said, "Yeah, a little."

Running Deer put his good hand behind his head and stared at Clint for a few minutes.

"Keep him alive, all right?" he said suddenly. "He's pigheaded, and he might want to do something foolish."

"Like kill the men when we find them?"

"Yeah, like that," Running Deer said.

"Tell me something, Running Deer."

"John."

"John," Clint said, "when you signed on with him—for whatever your reasons were—did you really expect to find these men?"

"Yeah," Running Deer said, "I did—I still do."

"And when you found them? What were you going to do then?"

"Whatever he wanted to do."

"Kill them?"

Running Deer shrugged.

"If that's what he wants."

"You two are good friends, huh?"

"We're friends."

"Well," Clint said, "I don't know if I can do that for him."

"Just keep him alive," Running Deer said, "that's all. If you want, *don't* find them. Leave that to me."

"What do you mean?" Clint asked. "Run him around in circles until you get back in the saddle?"

"If that's what it takes."

Clint scratched his chin and said, "I don't know if I can do that either."

"Well," John Running Deer said, "do what you can do, but—"

"I know," Clint said, holding up his hand, "keep him alive."

Chapter Twenty-Five

Clint was nursing a late beer in the Red Saddle when the batwing doors opened and Sheriff Roe Healy walked in.

"Adams," Healy said, joining him at the bar.

"Beer, Sheriff?" the bartender asked.

"Yeah, Tom."

"Looking for me, Sheriff?" Clint asked.

The sheriff accepted his beer from the bartender and took a sip before replying.

"No, Adams, I wasn't looking for you," he said. "I'm just making my rounds. What are you doing here? I thought you liked the Broken Wheel."

"They keep expecting me to shoot holes in the ceiling over there."

"Ah," Healy said. "I wonder why."

"Beats me."

"I don't recall if I asked you before how long you intend to be in town."

"So ask me now."

For some reason Clint had taken an instant dislike to Sheriff Healy earlier. Now he was being foolish and baiting the man.

The sheriff stared at him, then said, "How long do you intend to be in town?"

"I'll be leaving tomorrow morning, as a matter of fact," Clint said.

"Oh," Healy said, "too bad."

"I'll be back, though," Clint added. "I'm leaving my team and rig behind."

"You'll be back soon, then?"

"Can't say," Clint told him. "I don't really know."

"Well," Healy said, finishing his beer and setting the empty mug down on the bar, "try not to shoot any holes in this ceiling, huh?"

"I won't," Clint said. "In fact, I'm going to finish this beer and turn in."

"Good idea," Healy said.

Clint watched the man leave and then turned to the bartender.

"Does he always stop in for a beer here during his rounds?"

"Most of the time," the bartender said. "We like to stay on the sheriff's good side."

"Makes sense."

"You ain't gonna, are you?" the bartender asked.

"Gonna what?" Clint asked.

"Shoot holes in the ceiling?"

Clint looked up at the ceiling, which was already very pitted, either from age or from other weapons' discharges. In fact, there was one area that looked as if it had been peppered with a shotgun blast.

"Who'd notice?" Clint asked.

The bartender looked up and then looked at Clint and shrugged.

Clint finished his beer and left the place. Outside he could hear laughter and yelling coming from the Broken Wheel, but even if he could have gotten up a poker game over there he still didn't feel up to the crowd and the noise.

He finally decided to go along with what he had told the sheriff. He'd go to his hotel room and get some sleep, especially if that girl Betty kept her word and came to his room at three o'clock.

He had a feeling, just from looking at the girl and talking to her, that he was going to need all the rest he could get.

Chapter Twenty-Six

Clint heard the gentle knock on his door and rolled out of bed.

"Wow," she said as he opened the door.

"What?"

"I only had to knock once," she said, moving in past him. "You must be anxious."

"I'm looking forward to it, yeah," he said, closing the door.

He had left the wall lamp on low, and in the gentle yellow glow it was giving off he took a look at her. She had thrown a shawl over her working clothes, and now she removed it and dropped it to the floor so he could see her impressive cleavage.

"I've been working all night," she said apologetically. "I haven't had time to take a bath—"

"Never mind," he said, taking her into his arms. He knew what she meant. He could smell her perspiration, but the smell of a woman—her real smell—was not something he found offensive. In fact, it was working on him, exciting him. He held her close, but didn't kiss her yet.

"Ooh," she said, bumping her pelvis against his and feeling his erection there, "you are ready to go, aren't you?"

"Aren't you?" he asked.

"Mmm," she said, lifting her chin.

He lowered his face to hers, but didn't kiss her yet—not quite. He brushed his mouth near hers, then let his cheek touch hers lightly. His hands were on her bare back, and hers were around his waist. He could feel her body trembling. She was not as cool and calm as she would have liked him to think.

"You're trembling," he said in her ear.

"Okay," she said, "so I'm nervous. I haven't done this in a long time—I mean, given it away for free, you know?"

"Is there a difference?" he asked, kissing her ear, letting his tongue linger.

"Ooh," she said, "yes, there sure is. This is for my own pleasure . . . ohhh. . . ." He let his mouth wander down her cheek until he was kissing her neck, and then her shoulder. She suddenly shivered.

"What?"

"You're giving me the chills," she said. "God, kiss me already!"

He laughed, and kissed her, gently at first, just easing his tongue into her mouth. She responded just as gently, moaning, and then pulled her mouth away from his and looked up at him.

"Ooh," she said, "you have potential."

"For what?"

"For an interesting night," she said, hugging him tightly, "to say the least."

He moved his hand up her back until he found the clasp of her dress and undid it. She stepped back and let the dress fall to her waist. Her breasts, big and round and pale, almost glowed in the soft light of the lamp. Her nipples were dark brown, thick with wide aureola. The dress caught on her ample hips, and she wiggled them in order to let the dress fall to the floor. She stepped out of the dress and her shoes, and now all she wore was a wisp of white on her hips.

Clint went down on both knees and eased her underwear down so that she could step out of it. His face was close to her crotch, and he savored the smell of her before leaning in and kissing her there. She was wet and ready, and he kissed the lips of her vagina and pushed his tongue into her. She cried out, startled, and spread her legs. She put her hands on his shoulders as he continued to lick her.

"God," she moaned, "my legs . . ."

"What's wrong with your legs?" he asked. He ran one hand up her leg to her thigh, enjoying the smoothness of her pale flesh.

"They're weak," she said. "If we don't move to the bed, I'm gonna fall."

"Well, then," he said, giving her vagina one last kiss, "by all means let's move to the bed. . . ."

He stood up and surprised her by lifting her into his arms. She was a solid girl, heavy, but not too heavy for him.

"Are you trying to sweep me off my feet, Clint?" she asked.

He laughed.

"I thought that was what I just did, Betty."

He carried her to the bed and set her down gently on it.

"I want to watch you undress," she said.

"All right."

He had fallen asleep fully dressed, having removed only his gun and his boots. He took off his shirt now and reached for his pants, but she stopped him.

"Wait," she said.

She got to her knees on the bed facing him and unbuckled his trousers. He let the pants fall to the floor and kicked them away.

She put her hand on his hard penis through his underwear, then just pulled them down a bit in front so that the tip of his penis stuck out. She leaned over and ran her tongue over it and he moaned. She pulled the underwear down further and ran her tongue down further. Finally, his underwear dropped to the floor, and she cupped his testicles in her hands and kissed his lower belly, wetting him with her tongue.

"Lie down," she said. "Come on, lie down next to me. I want to enjoy this. My God, for the first time in a long time I really want to enjoy this."

He obliged her, lying down next to her, and she was true to her word for the rest of the night.

Chapter Twenty-Seven

Clint woke up, surprised that he had even fallen asleep. He looked out the window and saw that the sun was about to come up. He turned his head the other way and looked at Betty. She was lying on her belly. Her pillow, instead of being under her head, was beneath her belly. This hiked her ample butt up in the air some, which caused him to stir. He leaned over and ran his mouth over one cheek, and then the other. After that he ran his tongue down the crease between them. She moaned and stirred. He spread her cheeks and poked with his tongue. She started and jumped, and looked at him over her shoulder. She didn't move, though, and he continued to stroke her with his tongue until she said, "Ooh, that's enough, that's enough."

He stopped and looked up at her.

"I ain't never met a man like you," she said. "You do things . . . and don't you ever get tired?"

"I am tired," he said, "but I have to leave soon."

"What can I do for you?" she asked.

He bit her on the butt, and she shouted and

jumped, drawing her knees up and pulling her behind away from him.

"Wake me up," he said.

She pulled her knees up even further and rolled onto her back. Then she released her knees and spread her legs apart so that he could see her very clearly, pink and very wet.

"This wake you up, baby?"

He was awake.

Clint closed the door to his room softly, so as not to wake Betty. Before she fell asleep, though, he had told her that he'd be coming back for his team and his rig.

"You son of a bitch," she had said, but she was smiling. "You bad man. You got me into your bed under false pretenses, didn't you?"

"I did not," he said. "First of all I didn't promise anything."

"Maybe not," she said, reaching for him, "but you surely did deliver."

He walked over to the Doubletree Hotel and knocked on Stan Barton's door.

"Come on in."

He entered and saw Barton seated on the bed, fully dressed.

"Ready to go?" he asked.

"I'm ready," Barton said.

The ex-lawman had his gun belt on and his hat was on the bed next to him, for once not kicked halfway across the room. He stood up and reached for his saddlebags, which were also on the bed.

"Stan, can I ask you something?"

"Sure," Barton said, "why not?"

"Why the gun?" Clint asked. "If you're blind, why are you wearing the gun?"

"A man without a gun is a target, Clint," Barton said. "You know that. Especially a man who used to wear a tin star. From far off nobody knows I'm blind, but they'd know if I wasn't wearing a gun."

"I see," Clint said, but something else still puzzled him. Barton didn't want people to know he was blind, and yet he had insisted on telling his story to the newspapers. One seemed to contradict the other.

"Something else you want to ask me?"

"No, no," Clint said, "that was all."

"You know," Barton said, moving toward the door, avoiding the bed cleanly, "I have a real good sense of hearing. I mean, it even seems to have gotten better now that I'm blind. Sometimes, I can hit what I'm shooting at just by listening."

"By shooting at the sound?"

"That's right," Barton said, reaching the door and standing right next to Clint.

"The trouble with that is," Clint said, "how can you tell the sound a friend is making from the sound an enemy is making?"

Barton thought for a moment, and then said, "Yeah, I can see where that would be a problem."

Chapter Twenty-Eight

When they reached the livery stable Bill Adler was there, with both horses saddled and ready to go. The supplies Clint had bought had been split into two burlap sacks, one tied to the saddle of each horse. Since Barton and Running Deer had ridden into town without a pack animal, Clint assumed that Barton would want to leave the same way. When you were trailing someone, a pack animal only slowed you down.

"They're all ready," Adler said proudly.

"Thanks, Bill," Clint said.

"Hold on a minute," Barton said.

Clint and Adler watched as the blind man studied his new horse, using his hands. He walked completely around the animal, running his hands over the horse's chest, flanks, legs, examining the horse in every way he possibly could with his hands.

"A fine animal," he announced at last. "Not that I didn't trust you, Clint."

"Hey, no problem," Clint said. "You've certainly got a right to look over your own animal."

Adler made a face as Clint said "look over," but Clint knew what he was saying. He'd already decided that if he was going to have to watch what he said every step of the way, he'd be afraid to open his mouth.

"Let me take those," Clint said. He took Barton's saddlebags from him and secured them to the horse. "Can you mount?"

"Mount and dismount," Barton said. "There are still some things I can do for myself."

Clint watched as the blind man fitted his boot into the stirrup and mounted up. He then handed Barton his horse's reins.

"Take good care of my team, Bill," Clint said, climbing aboard Duke's broad back.

"I'll do that, Clint."

"And watch over my rig," Clint said. "I don't want to come back and find anything missing."

"Don't worry," Adler said, "you can trust me."

"I better be able to," Clint said, "I'm paying you enough for the privilege."

"And a fair price it is, too," the big blacksmith said with a smile.

"I'm just sorry I wasn't able to talk to Running Deer before I left," Barton said.

"I talked to him last night," Clint said.

"You did?"

"Yep," Clint said. "I told him that you and I would be leaving in the morning, and that you'd keep in touch by telegraph so that he'd know where we were at all times and could catch up when he was able."

"How did he take it?" Barton asked. "Being replaced by you, I mean."

"He gave me my instructions."

"Did he now?" Barton asked. "And just what did he tell you?"

"That you could be ornery at times," Clint said, "and that I should just ignore it as long as I could."

"And when you couldn't?"

"He said I should trip you."

"Hmph," Barton said. "What else did that heathen have to say?"

"Just that I was to keep you alive."

"Well," Barton said, "at least he got the last part right. How was he feeling?"

"Well," Clint said, "under the circumstances I think he was feeling pretty good."

"What circumstances?"

"That landlady of his has taken a real shine to him," Clint said. "I wouldn't be surprised if, with her nursing him, it didn't take him a little longer to heal than necessary."

John Running Deer sat up in bed, testing his shoulder. It hurt like the devil—more so because of the night's exertions.

Molly Mulligan was lying on the bed next to him, on her belly. He looked at her, the elegant line of her back, the gentle rise of her almost flat butt. Her breasts were so small that, lying on her belly, it looked as if she didn't even have any. Still, she had more energy and pure enjoyment of sex than any woman he had ever had before.

He stood up and walked to his window. He couldn't see the livery stable from here—hell, it was clear across town—but he imagined that he was watching Stan Barton and Clint Adams as they mounted up and prepared to leave town. He'd been riding with Barton for many months and had known him for years before that. There were times when Barton needed a posse and just couldn't get one. Those were the times he'd come to John Running Deer, and together they'd hunt down bank robbers, or killers, and do what had to be done when they caught up to them—which they always did. That was why Running Deer told Clint Adams that he expected to catch up to the three men who had killed Barton's family. If they didn't catch them, it would be the first time they failed as a team and—blind or not—he knew Barton would not stand for that.

"John?"

He turned and saw Molly watching him from the bed. She had barely moved, just lifted her head.

"What's wrong?" she asked.

"Nothing."

"What are you doing by the window?"

He turned and looked out the window again.

"Just wishing an old friend good luck."

Chapter Twenty-Nine

The first argument they had happened the first night that they camped. Clint spent most of the day learning how fast or slow to ride, where to ride—alongside or in front of Barton—when to talk and when not to talk. It seemed that there were times when Barton simply wanted to ride in silence, and other times when he liked to chat. Clint quickly learned that he was going to have to know when Barton felt like talking and when he didn't.

Clint was surprised at two things. One, that Barton rode so well, and two, that they made such good time. Of course, the second was a direct result of the first.

"You ride real well," Clint said at one point.

"I was a great rider before . . . before I lost my eyes," Barton said. "Now I just have to let the horse go where he wants to. He'll take me there."

"Where?"

"There," Barton said, and pointed ahead of them.

Clint wondered what would happen if Barton

got on a horse and just set out. Where would he end up?

Later, after they camped, Clint prepared a dinner of bacon and beans. When he had finished cleaning up, they had the argument.

"What do you mean I can't stand watch?" Barton said.

"I just meant . . . uh, that is . . ."

"I may not have eyes, Clint," Barton said, "but I still have ears."

"I just thought you'd like to rest—"

"I'm blind," Barton said, "I'm not crippled. I can stand watch as well as you can."

"Stan—"

"What's the moon like?" Barton asked.

"It's, uh, about a quarter."

"Not much light from it, huh?"

"No, not much."

"Look straight out and tell me what you see," Barton said.

Clint looked straight out from the camp and saw nothing but darkness.

"I see black," he said, beginning to get the idea.

"Now look into the fire."

"I can't do that, Stan."

"Why not?"

"It'll destroy my night vision," Clint said. "You know that."

"I don't have that problem, Clint."

"I know."

"I don't have any night vision to destroy," Barton said. "Are you starting to see?"

"Yes, I am," Clint said. "In a way, you'll be even better at keeping watch than I am."

"Oh, I know that's not so, Clint," Barton said. "I'm not foolish enough to believe that, but I think I've made my point. On a night like this—and on most nights—keeping watch is more hearing than seeing."

"Okay, okay," Clint said. "So I was wrong. Do you want the first watch, or the second?"

"I'll take the first," Barton said. "I won't notice when the sun comes up. See, there are some things you can do better than I can."

"I'm glad to hear it," Clint said. "I was beginning to worry."

Clint went to sleep without thinking to ask Barton how he'd know when it was time to wake him up for his watch. Still, Barton managed to wake him up at just the right time.

"I made coffee," Barton said.

Clint noticed that the ex-lawman was favoring his left hand.

"Not without paying the price, I see," he said.

Barton put the hand behind his back and said, "It's just a little burn."

Clint moved to the fire and poured himself a cup of coffee. It was strong, just the way he liked it.

"How is it?" Barton asked, and Clint told him it was fine. "I'll have a cup, too, before I turn in."

Clint poured the man a cup and handed it to him, and they sat near the fire to drink it.

"Can I ask you a question?"

"Wait," Barton said, "let me guess. What am I going to do after I've caught the men who killed my family?"

"That's the question."

"I don't know," Barton said. "I haven't thought that far in advance. Or maybe I don't want to think that far in advance. I mean, what will I be able to do? Sit in a rocker on some porch and wait for someone to bring me my meals?"

"Somehow I don't see you doing that," Clint said.

"Why not?"

"A man who gets on the back of a horse to hunt three killers, even though he can't see?" Clint said. "I think that man will find something to do with his life."

"Well, it's fine that you have so much confidence in me," Barton said. He tried to dump the remains of his coffee into the fire and missed. He put the empty cup down on the ground and got to his feet.

"Don't you?" Clint asked.

"No," Barton said, reaching for his saddle and his blanket, "no, I don't. To tell you the God's honest truth, Clint, I'm scared."

"Of what?"

He settled back against his saddle and covered himself with the blanket.

"This is all I know," he said. "Upholding the law, hunting a man when I have to. When this is over, I have no idea what I'll do."

"I'm sure there are a lot of things you can do," Clint said.

"Oh yeah?" Barton said. "Name one."

He gave Clint a few moments to come up with something, and when he didn't he rolled over and said, "Good night. Wake me good and early. Sleeping's not one of my favorite things."

Clint couldn't exactly blame him for that. Sleep brought dreams, and what dreams the man must have had.

Clint poured himself another cup of coffee and drank it thoughtfully. What was there that a blind man could do? A blind man with the qualifications of a lawman? There wasn't much call for a blind lawman, was there? What would he ever do, Clint wondered, if he went blind? All he did was ride around from place to place, looking to live his life. Blind, he would probably have to stay put, stay in one place all the time. How would his restless spirit accept that?

He couldn't imagine what it must be like to be blind. Once or twice during the ride that day he thought about asking Barton, but then decided that would be stupid—stupid and cruel. Still he wondered.

He looked up and out into the darkness and wondered what it must be like to see only that. Never see the sun, or the moon, or a pretty woman, a coyote, or even a buzzard. What would happen if suddenly you couldn't see all of the things you took for granted?

Maybe, he thought, it was time to stop taking those things for granted.

Chapter Thirty

Two days later they crossed into Colorado. The first town they came to was called Emoryville.

"Ever heard of it?" Clint asked, after reading the name aloud off a crude signpost.

"No," Barton said, "I can't say that I have. What's it say about the population?"

"It doesn't," Clint said. "I guess we won't know that until we get there."

"If it's a decent-sized town it may have a lawman who can help us," Barton said. "He might know something about the gang we're looking for."

"Only we're not sure if the gang you heard about is the gang you're looking for," Clint said.

"Well," Barton said, "I guess we'll find that out when we catch up to them, won't we?"

Emoryville turned out to be more of a ghost town than anything else. Most of the buildings were run-down and deserted, and Clint didn't see any sign of life until they reached the center of town. Here there seemed to be half a dozen buildings which had been kept up. If there were people living there, this was where they lived, in the center of town.

"What do you see?" Barton asked, and Clint described it to him. Another thing he was learning was to describe things to Barton exactly as he saw them.

"Sounds like the people who stayed decided they only needed a few buildings."

"Well," Clint said, "let's find out if there *are* any people here."

They rode up to the front of one of the better-looking buildings, which happened to be the hotel.

"Come inside with me," Clint said.

"I'll wait here," Barton said, stepping up onto the boardwalk.

"Stan—"

"You go ahead," Barton said, "I'm not going anywhere. Go on!"

"All right!"

Clint felt a momentary annoyance with the man, then remembered what John Running Deer had said about him and let it go.

He went into the hotel and was surprised to find that the inside was dust-free. There was no one there, but it was clear that there had been recently, and whoever they were, they were keeping the place clean.

The hotel used to have a dining room, but that part of it had not been so well kept up. There were tables and chairs, but some of the chairs were piled atop the tables while others just lay on their sides on the floor gathering dust.

Clint went back through the lobby to join Barton outside.

"No one there," Clint said.

"I think there is."

"What?"

"I heard someone."

"Where?"

"Shh."

Barton listened, and so did Clint.

"Hear that?" Barton said.

"What?" Clint asked, hearing nothing.

"Quiet," Barton said. "Just listen."

They both stood stock-still, listening. Clint even tried not to breath so he could hear what the blind man was hearing.

And then he did.

Whistling.

Someone was whistling.

"Whistling?" Clint asked softly.

"That's it."

"Where's it coming from?"

Barton pointed to the sky and said, "Up."

"Up?" Clint said. "Up where?"

"Upstairs, Clint," Barton said. "Upstairs."

"Oh," Clint said, "upstairs in the hotel."

For a moment he'd thought . . . but that was dumb. He could hear the whistling plain as day now, and then realized that it was coming closer.

"Inside," he said, and went back into the hotel.

There the whistling was loud, and now he saw the source. A man was coming down the steps, and he was whistling a tune Clint didn't know.

"Hello," Clint said.

The man stopped whistling abruptly and clutched at his heart. He was dressed in a clean white shirt, black pants, and a red and

118   J. R. ROBERTS

black vest. He appeared to be about sixty, and he had a well-groomed white beard.

"Jesus be saved!" he said. "You scared the livin' daylights out of me."

"I'm sorry," Clint said. He heard Barton enter the lobby behind him. "I didn't mean to frighten you."

"Didn't," the old man said, coming the rest of the way down the steps. "Just surprised me, is all."

"But you just said—"

"Never mind what I just said," the man said, moving around behind the desk. "You fellas want rooms?"

"You have rooms?" Clint asked, obviously surprised.

The man stared at him as if he was crazy and said, "This is a hotel, ain't it? Ain't that what it says on the outside?"

"Well, yes, but—"

"Then you either wants rooms," the man said, "or you don't. Which is it? Huh? Which is it?"

Clint peered at the man intently, trying to decide if *he* was crazy or not.

Barton came up next to him and said softly, "Is he mad?"

"I can't tell," Clint said. "Maybe."

"Speak up, speak up," the man said. "You have to tell me what you want. I can't read minds, and I'm late."

"Late for what?"

The man stared at Clint, puzzled for a moment, then shook his head and said, "I'm just late, is all. Do you want rooms?"

"Are they clean?" Clint asked.

"Of course they're clean," the man said. "What do ya think I was doin' when you got here? I was cleanin' 'em."

"We need some rest," Barton said, "and I wouldn't mind a bed after three days in the saddle."

"Might as well," Clint said. Then he turned to the old man before he could holler at them again. "Okay, we'll take two rooms."

"Well, it's about time," the man said. "What takes a body so long to make up his mind?"

"We've been riding for quite a few days," Clint said. "Guess my manners got rusty."

"That's all right, young feller," the man said. "Just come on over here and sign the register and I'll give you two nice rooms. Nicest ones in the house. As it happens, we're a little empty these days, but things'll pick up. They'll pick up."

Clint moved to the register and signed his name and Barton's. As he did so, he noticed the man's hands. They were covered with cuts, some fresh, some scabbed over. Where there were no cuts or scabs there were scars and blisters.

"Does, uh, anyone else live in town?" Clint asked.

"No, nobody else," the man said. "Just me."

"Just you?"

"That's what I said."

"But the buildings," Clint said. "The ones next to you, and across from you, they're pretty well kept up."

"They should be," the man said. "I keep them up."

"By yourself?"

The man took two keys down off the wall behind him and turned to stare at Clint.

"Well, if I live here by myself then I keep up the buildings by myself, don't I?"

"I suppose so," Clint said, accepting the keys.

"Got any bags you want me to carry up?"

"Uh, no," Clint said, "just saddlebags. I, uh, don't suppose there's a livery stable around?"

"End of the street," the man said, "but you'll have to unsaddle 'em and bed 'em down yourself. I can't do it. I'm late."

"So you said," Clint said. "We'll take care of the horses ourselves."

"Good, good."

As the man started around the desk Clint said, "By the way, what's your name?"

"Emory," the man said.

"Like the town?" Barton asked.

"Exactly like the town," Emory said. "It should be. After all, I named it."

"What was it called before it was called Emory-ville?" Barton asked.

The man stopped, stared at them a moment, and then said, "I'm late. You'll have to excuse me. I'm late." And he scurried out the front door.

"Late for what?" Barton asked.

"I don't know," Clint said. "How can he be the late for anything if he's the only one who lives here?"

"I don't know," Barton said.

"We better take care of the horses," Clint said. "Then we can check out our rooms."

Chapter Thirty-One

Although the structure of the livery stable was run-down, the inside was clean. There was also feed and bales of hay.

"This isn't right," Clint said.

"What?" Barton asked.

"There's too much stuff here," Clint said. "Feed, hay, and how does this fella Emory eat if he's the only one here? Where does he get food? And water? And clothing?"

"Maybe he also kept the general store up," Barton said.

"Maybe, but where is he getting the stock?"

"I see what you mean."

Clint started unsaddling Duke while Barton did the same thing to his horse. It was something he could always have done blindfolded, so doing it blind was no problem.

"Someone must be bringing him things," Barton said, removing the saddle from the horse's back.

"Right," Clint said, removing Duke's saddle.

"Bringing him the supplies he needs to keep his buildings up."

"Is he doing that work himself, do you think?" Barton asked.

"Oh yeah," Clint said. "I saw his hands. They're a mess, probably from the carpentry."

"So what are they getting in return?" Barton wondered aloud.

"How about a place to hide out?"

"You're saying they're outlaws."

"Maybe," Clint said.

"Well, maybe we can find something out from Emory," Barton said.

"I don't know," Clint said, "it seems like whenever we want to know something, he says he's late. I think he just *may* be mad."

"Or," Barton said, "he wants us to think he is."

"What makes you say that?"

"Just the sound of his voice," Barton said. "There's something about it, something false."

"Like he's . . . acting?"

"Maybe," Barton said.

"Well," Clint said, "we could ask him."

"Or you could keep an eye on him, follow him," Barton said.

"That would take time," Clint said. "We only want to stay here overnight."

"We do," Barton said, "unless this is where the gang we're looking for hides out."

"Right near the border, you mean," Clint said. "With easy access to Wyoming."

"It's a possibility."

"It's also a possibility that there is *a* gang hiding

out here, but not the one we're looking for."

"Well, as you've said before," Barton said, "there's one way to find out."

They finished caring for their horses and walked back to the hotel.

"Do you think he noticed I'm blind?" Barton asked.

"If he's mad, maybe not," Clint said. "If he's sane, maybe."

"Well, maybe he's sane, but just a little off in the head," Barton said. "It'd be a help right now if he didn't notice."

"Well, the only way we'd be able to keep it from him would be for you to stay in the room."

"If you're going to follow him," Barton said, "then that's where I'm going to have to stay, otherwise I'll just get in the way."

"I don't like leaving you alone," Clint said.

"In the room," Barton said, "I'll be fine."

Clint remembered how Barton had gotten the drop on him in his room back in Liberty—but he also remembered that he could have gotten away if he'd wanted to. He also felt he could have disarmed Barton.

"I'll take you upstairs and take a turn around town," Clint said. "Maybe I'll see something helpful."

"I don't like letting you go out without someone to watch your back," Barton said. "If there *is* a gang in town somewhere—"

"It can't be helped," Clint said. "We could both stay in the room, but if there is a gang holed up here, we could be in trouble."

"Why don't we just leave, then?" Barton asked.

"Because," Clint reminded him, "it might be the gang you're looking for."

"I hope it is," Barton said.

"There's something you haven't told me, Stan."

"What's that?"

"Who I'm looking for," Clint said. "Can you describe any of the men who . . . who shot you?"

"Oh yes," Barton said. "There's something about the last thing you see before you're blinded, I think. The last thing I saw was their faces, all three of them. They're burned into my mind, Clint. I can describe each of them for you perfectly."

They were approaching the hotel.

"Okay, then," Clint said, "let's get upstairs and you can do just that."

Chapter Thirty-Two

They dropped Clint's saddlebags off in his room, and then he walked Barton over to his. Both rooms were laid out the same, beds with mattresses as thin as blankets and no other furniture other than a chair.

"At least it's clean," Barton said.

"How can you tell?"

"Smells clean," the blind man said. "I been in some rooms that just downright smelled dirty."

Clint looked around. Barton was right; for the most part the room was clean—cleaner, anyway, than a lot he'd been in.

Both rooms overlooked the main street. Clint walked to the window to look outside.

"See anything?" Barton asked.

"Nothing."

"I wonder where our friend went," Barton said.

"That's easy," Clint said, coming back from the window, "he went to wherever it was he was late gettin' to."

"Right."

"You want to give me those descriptions now?" Clint asked.

"I will," Barton said, "but you got to understand, this is gonna be like reliving the whole thing for me. I've got to do it that way in order to bring the faces to mind good and sharp."

"Stan, if it—"

"It'll be painful, sure," Barton said, "but it's got to be done. You got to know who you're looking for."

"I suppose," Clint said. "Just go ahead and start when you're ready. . . ."

Stan Barton looked over at the stove, where his wife, Martha, stood cooking dinner. She'd been standing at that stove—or a stove like it—for fourteen years now, and every time he looked at her he loved her more.

"Where's Jimmy?" he asked.

"Doing his chores," she said over her shoulder. "He'll be here for dinner. He doesn't ever miss dinner, does he?"

"No, he sure doesn't," Barton said.

"A lot like his poppa in that way, isn't he?" Martha asked.

Jimmy was twelve and did most of the chores around the house while his father was doing his job as the marshal of Cobb County. The house was just outside of the town of Park City. Although the town was far from being a city, Barton had been marshal there for five years now, ever since he, Martha, and Jimmy had moved there so he could take the job. He got the house as part of the job of marshal.

Barton washed his hands and face in a basin of water then turned and watched as Martha set the table. She was a handsome woman in her late thirties. She didn't have dance hall looks, but to Stan Barton she was much more substantial than that. She was the loveliest, gentlest creature he had ever met, and he was constantly amazed at the fact that she loved him.

"Pa!" Jimmy's voice called from outside.

"What's that boy shouting about?" Martha said, walking toward the door.

"Pa!" Jimmy shouted again. "Riders."

"Martha," Barton said, "I'll take a look—" But she was already heading for the door.

. Before she could get to it, though, Jimmy slammed it open and stepped inside.

"Pa," he said, his blond hair down in his eyes, "riders comin'. Three of 'em."

Barton's gun belt was hanging on a peg on the wall, but he moved to the door without it, mostly to keep Jimmy and Martha from going outside.

"Wait," he said, "both of you." But they were already going out the door as he heard the horses approach the house.

He hurried to the door behind them and was just stepping outside when the shooting started. His first instinct was to go for his gun, but it was hanging on the wall.

He heard Martha scream as the bullets struck her and sent her reeling back into him. He put his arms out to catch her, and a bullet struck him in the shoulder. That combined with her deadweight pulled him to the ground, where another bullet struck him, this time in the hip.

On the ground he saw Martha's face, and her eyes were wide and sightless. She was dead, he knew. Beyond her he could see Jimmy, also lying on the porch. His blond hair was covered with blood.

He looked up, then, at the three riders and imprinted their faces in his mind. Then one of them, one with a scar across his face, rode closer and aimed at Barton's head. Barton tried to move, but he was pinned by his wife's body. Then there was a shot, and his vision went red, then black, and his eyes felt like they were on fire. The bullet had narrowly missed the bridge of his nose, but the powder had burned his eyes, blinding him. He never heard them ride off, only his own screaming until he passed out.

"The first one," Barton said darkly, "had a scar across his face—right across his face, from the bottom of his left eye, across the bridge of his nose, right down to the right corner of his mouth. The second one was young, maybe eighteen or nineteen, and he was laughing. I noticed that he was missing both front teeth. The third one was wearing a red bandanna, and he had long hair, black as coal, and a long, droopy mustache the same color."

Clint let out his breath, surprised that he had been holding it. Could he have been holding it for the length of the entire story?

"That's them, Clint," Barton said, his voice steady. "If you see them, you'll know them."

Clint started to reply and found that he had to clear his throat before doing so.

"Yes, Stan," he said, "I'll know them."

"You see them," Barton said, "don't go after them alone, you hear? You come back and tell me about it. I'll help you with them."

"Stan—"

"I don't know how," Barton went on, and now his voice wasn't so steady, "and I don't know what I can do, but I'll help you with them. I swear I will."

"All right, Stan," Clint said, "all right. If I see them, I'll come back and let you know."

"Don't go getting yourself killed, you hear?" Barton said. "I could be sitting up here forever if that happens."

"I'll keep that in mind," Clint said. "I promise, Stan."

Chapter Thirty-Three

When Clint got down to the lobby their host, Emory—if that was really his name—was still nowhere to be seen. He stepped outside in front of the hotel and looked up and down the street, but there was nothing to see. He tried taking a page out of Barton's book. He stood still and listened intently, but all he could hear was the wind. For all intents and purposes, Emoryville looked like a ghost town. Even if one person was still living there and—incredibly—keeping a small, center section of the town alive, it still qualified as a ghost town as far as Clint was concerned.

He looked both ways then decided to walk back toward the livery stable. He remembered passing an abandoned newspaper office along the way. Maybe he'd find something to read that would tell him something about the town.

When he reached the newspaper office, he saw that the legend on the window said CARLYLE REGISTER. Apparently, before the old man renamed the town, it had been called Carlyle. Clint dug into his memory, but couldn't pull anything to surface that had to do with a town called Carlyle.

He was about to try the front door when he got an uncomfortable feeling about the horses. What if Emory—or someone else—had taken them? Then Clint and Barton would be trapped in town. Of course, Duke would not be easy to take, but they might have been far enough away from the livery not to have heard a commotion.

He left the newspaper office and went over to the livery. As he entered, he saw Duke standing in his stall. When he checked on Barton's horse, the animal was also in its stall. Now he was nervous about leaving the two animals alone there. Still, there was no way he could stand watch over them and still take a look at the town. If there was someone else in town besides Emory—especially if it was some sort of outlaw gang—then he wanted to know about it. He was going to have to trust the horses on their own.

He went up to Duke, patted his massive neck, and instructed him to stay. If someone came along and tried to remove the big gelding from the livery, they'd be in for a hell of a fight.

Reluctantly, Clint left the livery and walked back to the newspaper office. The front door was locked, but a good hard push was all it took to pop the lock and open the door. As he stepped inside, a musty smell assaulted his nostrils. It appeared that no one had been inside for a long time.

He closed the door behind him and started to look around. The floor was covered with old editions of the paper, and the old printing press was dusty and covered with dried ink that was so black it looked like dried blood.

Clint kept picking up old issues of the paper off the floor and checking the dates. When he found something close to the present date, he put it aside. Finally, he had a small stack of newspapers that were dated approximately five months earlier. He read some of the old headlines:

CARLYLE ON VERGE OF DYING!
BANK OF CARLYLE CLOSES!
COMMERCE DESERTS CARLYLE!
GANG INVADES CARLYLE!

The most recent newspaper had a headline that read:

LAST NAIL IN COFFIN. CARLYLE DIES!

He went back to the headline about the gang and read the story. Apparently, a gang of men had decided to use the dying town as their hideout, or headquarters. Their presence was driving out the last of the businessmen, until there was no one left, no residents, and no businesses.

Except for the old man, Clint thought, old Emory.

What if, he thought, Emory was simply kept around to keep a small section of the town up? The section that the gang would use when they were there? The question remained, then, was the gang there now? Probably not. When they were there, they probably used the livery; that was why the inside of the stable was kept up.

That meant that he had to get Duke and Barton's horse out of the stable before the gang could return. If they came back and saw the horses, Clint and Barton would be in trouble.

He left the newspaper office and looked up and down the street. Still no sign of anyone, but he now felt sure that the old man was the only person in town besides himself and Barton. Whatever Emory was doing, he was probably doing it in anticipation of the gang returning.

Clint hurried to the livery stable to move Duke and Barton's horse.

Chapter Thirty-Four

Once he had found a different place to leave their horses and their gear, Clint went back to the hotel. When he entered, he saw that the old man was not behind the desk. He hurried upstairs to check on Barton.

He knocked on the door, and Barton answered.

"See anybody?" the blind man asked.

"No," Clint said, "but I read some newspapers."

He told Barton what he had read in the old issues of the paper.

"Why would a gang continue to use this as a hideout if the newspaper *said* it was their hideout?" Barton asked when Clint finished.

"It was a small-town newspaper," Clint said, "published for the benefit of the townspeople. I don't think anyone outside of Carlyle ever read it."

"Carlyle," Barton repeated thoughtfully.

"Does the name ring a bell?"

"Almost," Barton said, "but I can't place it."

"Well, don't worry about it," Clint said. "If it's

134

there, it'll come back. Meanwhile, I moved the horses and gear."

"To where?"

"The south end of town. I found an abandoned feed and grain warehouse. I put them in there."

"Okay," Barton said, "that'll keep the gang from knowing we're here when they return—unless they talk to Emory."

"Right," Clint said. "We've got to do something about that old man."

"Like what?"

"I don't know," Clint said. "We've got to keep him from telling the gang we're here."

"You know," Barton said, "if we're going to wait for this gang to come back, we could be here a long time."

"Maybe," Clint said, "maybe not."

"What do you mean?"

"All that talk the old man was doing about being late," Clint said. "I think the gang is over-due now. I think he's trying to get things ready for them."

"Okay, so we're back to what do we do about him," Barton said.

"We can take him out of the play."

"You don't mean kill him?"

"No," Clint said forcefully, "not kill him, just put him out of action for a while. Tie him up, or lock him up somewhere."

"Won't they be curious when they arrive and he's not here?"

"Probably," Clint said, "but by that time we will have had a look at them. If they're the men we want, then we'll take them."

"And if they're not the men we want?" Barton said. "If they're some other gang?"

"Well, then, I say we get out of town without letting them know we were here," Clint said. "If they're not the gang we're looking for, then there's no sense getting involved with them."

"But if they are a gang—"

"You're not a lawman anymore, Stan," Clint reminded the man. "If they're wanted, then some lawman will catch them, eventually—but not us. We've got other fish to fry . . . don't we?"

"Yes," Barton said, "we do."

He clearly wasn't happy with the idea of letting a gang go off scot-free, though. The lawman in him was dying hard.

"Okay," Clint said, "I'm going to go out again and see if I can find Emory. I'll be back soon."

"Right."

"Don't open the door unless you hear my voice."

"I know that!" Barton said. Then he softened his voice and said, "Don't worry about me."

"I'm not worried about you," Clint said, "I'm worried about me. If I let anything happen to you, I'll have to answer to John Running Deer."

"Well, there's one way to make sure that nothing happens to me," Barton said.

"What's that?"

"Take me with you."

"Stan—"

"If I'm with you, Clint, you won't have to worry about me," Barton said. "Also, I might hear or smell something that you won't."

Clint turned away from the door and stared at the blind man for a few moments.

"Stan, if I take you with me you have to promise me some things."

"What's that?"

"You'll do what I say when I say it," Clint said.

"Fine."

"Even if I push you in a corner and tell you to stay there."

"Okay."

The man was agreeing too easily.

"A likely story."

"I'll cooperate, Clint," Barton said, "but we better get moving. What happens if that gang gets here before we're ready?"

He was right.

"Okay," Clint said, "but I'm warning you, if you don't do what I say, I'll knock you cold and roll you under a table . . . or something."

"Sure," Barton said, coming toward the door, "whatever."

Chapter Thirty-Five

This time when Clint went down to the lobby and saw that Emory still wasn't there, he decided to check the kitchen.

"Wait here," he told Barton, "behind the desk."

"Well, put me there then," Barton said, gritting his teeth.

Clint moved Barton around behind the desk and then went through the dining room to check the kitchen. It occurred to him that if a gang was using this as a hideout, they'd have to eat. The kitchen, however, was as deserted as the dining room. If they were eating, they were doing it in another building. But which one?

"Nobody in the kitchen," Clint said, "but the gang's got to eat."

"Someplace else then," Barton said, "like a saloon?"

"Let's check it out."

They went out the front door and stopped.

"Wait," Barton said. But this time instead of listening he did something else—he sniffed at the air.

Sure enough, there it was, the smell of food cooking. Even Clint could smell it. It had to be one of the buildings that the old man had been keeping up. Also, it made sense for one of those buildings to be a saloon, which probably had a kitchen.

Clint looked across the street, where three buildings stood in a better state of repair than any of the others around them. One of them had the batwing front doors of a saloon, although there was no sign on it.

"Looks like a saloon across the street," he said, taking Barton's arm. "Come on."

They walked across the street and approached the building carefully. When they reached the batwing doors, Clint peered over them. Sure enough, the inside had been kept up. It was clean, and there were five or six tables with four chairs at each. The bar, too, was clean, and on the shelves behind it were bottles of whiskey. Clint wondered if there was beer, too. He was suddenly very thirsty.

"This looks like it," Clint said.

"I hope so," Barton said. "I'm thirsty—and hungry, too."

They went inside, and the smell of food cooking was stronger.

"Jesus," Barton said in a low voice, "my stomach is growling."

"Well, keep it quiet."

Apparently the thing Emory was afraid of being late with was the gang's food.

Clint followed his nose to a door just off the end of the bar, Barton trailing along behind him.

From behind the door he heard someone humming and the sound of pots and pans. He suddenly smelled coffee. Now he didn't know what he wanted more, coffee or beer.

"I'm going in," Clint said, and Barton nodded. "Get behind the bar."

"Clint—"

"Behind the bar, Stan!" Clint hissed between his teeth.

Reluctantly, Barton moved around behind the bar, and Clint went into the kitchen.

The old man, Emory, was standing in front of a stove that had three pots on it, plus a pot of coffee. He was wearing an apron.

"Smells good," Clint said.

Emory spun around real fast and glared at Clint.

"What are you doin' here?" he demanded.

"We were hungry," Clint said. "Thought we'd hunt up some food."

"This food ain't for you," Emory said.

"Who's it for, Emory?"

The old man opened his mouth to answer, then snapped it shut.

"None of your business. You don't belong here. Go back to the hotel."

"Can't do that, Emory," Clint said. "My friend and I are hungry, and thirsty, and we've got some questions for you."

"I ain't answering any questions," Emory said, his lower jaw jutting out pugnaciously.

"Yes, Emory," Clint said, "you are."

"I can't—"

"But first we're going to eat," Clint said. "Is it ready?"

Chapter Thirty-Six

Clint used a big wooden spoon to fill two bowls with food and then had Emory carry them out into the saloon. He got Barton from behind the bar and sat him at a table.

"Do you have beer?" he asked Emory.

"Yeah."

"Get two," Clint said. "And Emory . . ."

"Yeah?"

"If you make a break for the door," Clint said, "I'll shoot you in the leg."

"I ain't makin' a break," the old man said. "You'll be in trouble soon enough."

"Jesus," Barton said around a mouthful of beef stew, "this guy's a good cook."

Clint tasted the food and agreed. It was possibly the best beef stew he'd ever had. Barton was enjoying it, too, because it was chunks of meat with vegetables, so there was nothing for him to have to cut.

"This is what you should order all the time," Clint said, "instead of just vegetables."

Barton's head lifted, and it was as if he was staring right at Clint.

"Why didn't I ever think of that?"

Emory came back with two beers and said, "What else do you want?"

"Sit down with us," Clint said. "We want to talk."

"About what?" the old man asked, sitting.

"About all of this," Clint said, "the accommodations, the food. Who brings it here? Who's it all for?"

"You'll find out soon enough," Emory said.

"Well, I'd like to find out sooner than that," Clint said. "Besides, they're late, aren't they?"

Emory's eyes widened for a moment, and then he caught himself.

"Who's late?" he asked.

"Them," Clint said. "The men you're cooking for. The gang that took over this town when it was still called Carlyle. It was nice of them to let you rename the town after yourself, wasn't it, Emory?"

The old man stuck his jaw out again and said, "It's a good name."

"It's a fine name, Emory," Clint said, "a fine name—and speaking of names, who are we waiting for?"

"Nobody."

"Come on," Clint said, "we know you're waiting for someone, we just don't know who."

"I ain't talkin'," Emory said. Suddenly, he looked as if something had just occurred to him. "You're law, ain't ya?"

"Does he look like the law, Emory?" Clint asked, pointing to Barton.

Emory looked at Barton, and for the first time he saw that the man was blind.

"He can't see?" the old man asked, in awe.

"That's right, Emory," Clint said, "he can't see. But he can hear well enough to shoot you in the leg before you make the door."

Emory looked at Clint and said, "Go on. . . ."

"It's true," Clint said. "He can shoot what he hears. Hits it every time."

"Go on . . ." Emory said again, looking at Barton with his mouth open. "Can you?" he asked Barton.

"Why don't you try for the door," Barton said, "and we'll find out."

Emory looked at Clint, who just shrugged his shoulders, and then back at Barton.

"Well?" the blind man asked.

"I ain't tryin' for the door," Emory said. "I'm just waitin'. I can be patient."

"Okay then," Clint said, "tell us who we're waiting for."

Emory didn't reply.

"He's not talking," Clint said to Barton.

"Make him talk," Barton said.

Clint studied Emory for a while and then said, "Naw, you make him talk."

"How?" Barton asked.

"Are you ready for a little target practice?" Clint asked. He looked at Emory and said, "If he doesn't practice, he gets rusty."

"Practice?"

"Sure," Clint said. "Emory, go stand over there by that wall."

"Wait a minute—"

"You going to talk?"

The old man glared at him and then compressed his lips tightly.

"Okay then," Clint said, "go over and stand by that wall like I said."

Emory hesitated, then stood up and went and stood with his back against the far wall.

Barton leaned over and said in a low voice, "What am I supposed to do now?"

"I'll stand you directly opposite him," Clint replied. "You can shoot anywhere but straight ahead. Okay?"

Barton looked amused by the idea and said, "Well, all right."

Chapter Thirty-Seven

Clint and Barton made Emory stand against the wall while they finished eating, letting the old man think things over for a while.

They washed their meal down with cold beer, and then Clint pushed away from the table.

"What about it, Emory?" Clint asked. "Ready to talk to us?"

"I ain't talkin'," the old man said.

Clint shrugged and said, "Suit yourself."

He walked around the table and got Barton to his feet. They made it look as if Barton couldn't even stand up by himself.

"Okay, Stan, stand right here," Clint said, positioning Barton directly across from Emory, who was swallowing hard.

"Okay," Clint said. "Emory, say something so he knows where you are."

The old man opened his mouth to answer, then got a crafty look on his face and kept his mouth closed.

"If you don't make some kind of noise, he won't know where you are," Clint said.

Emory looked smug and kept quiet.

"Okay, Stan," Clint said, "you'll have to guess where he is."

"I'll try and smell him," Barton said helpfully.

Clint backed away until he was leaning against the bar then said, "Okay, go ahead."

Barton drew his gun and fired, missing Emory by a good ten feet. Emory, however, had his eyes closed and couldn't see that Barton was firing wildly, into the ceiling, into the floor. The old man took it as long as he could, and then Clint drew his gun and fired one careful shot. The bullet whizzed past the old man's ear and struck the wall behind him.

"Wait, wait!" Emory shouted, thinking that the blind man had fired the shot.

Barton stopped shooting, ejected the spent shells, and began reloading.

"Was that you, Emory?" Clint asked. His gun was back in his holster before the old man opened his eyes.

"Don't let him shoot no more," Emory said.

He raised his hand to touch his ear and see if it was still there, then turned to look at the bullet hole in the wall. Sweat was running down his face, soaking his shirt beneath his arms.

"You ready to talk, Emory?" Clint asked.

"I—I need a beer," Emory said. "Then I'll tell ya what ya want to know."

"Okay," Clint said, "get yourself a beer."

While the old man went behind the bar for a beer, Clint touched Barton's arm and moved him back to the table.

"How'd I do?" Barton asked.

"Great," Clint said, "you hit the ceiling, the floor and—"

"Look out!" Barton shouted.

He turned, put his left arm out, and pushed Clint away from him violently. Clint, falling to the floor, watched as the blind man drew his gun and fired toward the bar.

Behind the bar Emory stood with a gun. Barton fired three times, and two bullets struck Emory in the chest, driving him back against the shelves of liquor. The third bullet shattered a bottle on the wall. As Emory fell to the floor, an avalanche of bottles followed him down from the shelves.

Barton stood there waving his gun, yelling, "Clint? Clint? Did I get him? Did I get him?"

Clint got up off the floor slowly, staring at Barton in awe. He walked to the bar and looked behind it. Emory was lying on the floor, covered with blood and whiskey.

Clint turned and looked at Barton, who still had his gun out and his head cocked to one side, listening.

"You got him."

Clint walked around the bar and leaned over the fallen Emory. The man had two bullets square in the center of his chest—fired by a blind man! There was broken glass all over the place, and the smell of whiskey was strong, mixed with blood. On the floor next to Emory's hand was an old Navy Colt. Clint picked it up and checked it. It was loaded and in working condition.

He stood up and looked at Barton.

"How did you know?" he asked.

"I heard the hammer cock," Barton said.

"I didn't hear anything."

"We were talking," Barton said, "but I heard it plain as day. I reacted by reflex. I—I hit him?"

"You hit him," Clint said, "twice, right in the chest, Stan. That was the most amazing thing I ever saw."

He came back around the bar and fronted Barton.

"You can put your gun away now," he said, and the blind man holstered the weapon.

"I think I need a drink," Barton said. Clint noticed that his hands were shaking.

"Yeah," Clint said. "So do I."

Chapter Thirty-Eight

Clint brought two glasses and a bottle of whiskey to the table. He poured and pushed one glass across to Barton.

"Easy," Clint said.

Barton nodded, felt for the glass, and lifted it to his mouth.

"Let me have your gun," Clint said.

Barton took it out of his holster without question and handed it over. Clint eased the cylinder out, ejected the three spent rounds for Barton, and handed it back to the blind man.

"Go ahead and reload it," Clint said. "I'm going to move the body."

"Okay."

Clint went behind the bar, grabbed the old man by the ankles, and pulled him along into the kitchen and through it into a back hallway. He left the body there and went back into the saloon. Barton had poured himself another drink and was tossing it down.

Clint sat opposite him and said, "Want something else to eat?"

Barton made a face and said, "No."

"I didn't say thanks," Clint said. "You probably saved my life."

Stan Barton thought about that and then suddenly smiled.

"Ironic, huh?" he said.

"Oh yeah," Clint said, nodding emphatically, "I'd say it was ironic."

"Bet you're glad now you didn't leave me in the room, huh?"

Clint just smiled and shook his head.

"Maybe *I* should have stayed in the room," Clint said. "That was damned careless of me."

"I don't know," Barton said. "My guess is the man didn't look like much of a threat—and he was behind there before and didn't go for the gun. He didn't figure to have one hidden back there."

"Doesn't matter," Clint said. "I didn't stay alive all these years by being careless. Want another drink?"

"Not whiskey," Barton said, wiping his mouth. "Maybe another beer."

"Yeah," Clint said, "me, too."

Chapter Thirty-Nine

"What do we do now?"

"Well," Clint said, staring at Barton over his beer, "I don't see that anything's changed, really. The old man's out of the way, and all we have to do is wait for the gang to get here."

"Yeah, but wait where?" Barton asked. "We can't just sit here."

"No," Clint said, "we have to be someplace where we—uh, I—can see them when they ride in. If they're the ones we want, then we'll have to decide how to play it."

"How else will we play it?" Barton asked. A muscle in his jaw was twitching. "If it's them, we take them."

Clint studied the man for a few moments and then decided that it was time for some truths.

"Look, Stan," he said, "there's something I have to say here."

"Okay," Barton said, "go ahead and say it."

"When you talk about taking them," Clint said, "what you're really talking about is *me* taking them."

"Wait a minute—"

"No," Clint said, "in spite of what happened here—and that was great, really, it was unbelievable—what use would you be to me out on the street?"

"Clint—"

"In the middle of a gunfight," Clint went on, "how are you going to hear a hammer click? Huh?"

"Clint—"

"And we have no idea how many of them there will be when they do get here," Clint went on. "If it's just the three who killed your family, well fine—but what if they ride in here with a dozen men? Then what? You and me against them? Two guns?"

"Clint," Barton said, "can I talk?"

"Sure," Clint said, "go ahead and talk."

"You're right," Barton said, "I know you're right. I wouldn't be any use to you in the middle of any kind of gun battle."

Clint stared at Barton, surprised the man was admitting this.

"I'll play this any way you want to," Barton said, "because you're right, you're the one who would have to do the most work. Your ass would be on the line, so you tell me how you want to play it, and that's what we'll do."

"All right," Clint said, still thrown off balance by the man's ready agreement. "All right, then, here's what we'll do. If there are more than just the three of them, we'll leave and go for help. At least we'll know where they're holed up."

"They won't be holed up here much longer,"

Barton pointed out, "not after they find Emory."

"Good point," Clint said, "but at least we'll know where they were last. All we have to do is ride to the nearest town for some law."

"Unless the nearest town is just like this," Barton said.

"Okay, yeah, then we have a problem. We have to find a town with a lawman and a telegraph line."

"Okay, fine," Barton said, "that's what we do if there are more than three. Now what do we do if there's just the three of them?"

"Well," Clint said, "if there's just three of them, then we'll probably be able to take them ourselves."

"You mean you'll be able to take them."

"I mean," Clint said, "that I can try."

"Have you ever faced three men at once before?" Barton asked. "I mean, I know your reputation and all, but we both know what reputations are worth, don't we?"

"Yes, we do," Clint said. "To answer your question, I have faced three men before."

"Well," Barton said, "obviously you came out on top, didn't you?"

"Uh," Clint said, "not without a lot of luck."

"Well sure," Barton said, "luck always has a lot to do with it."

There was a moment of silence and then Clint asked, "What about you?"

"What about me?"

"Ever face three men before?"

"Oh, yeah," Barton said, "once or twice. I used to be pretty good with a gun, when I had to be."

Remembering how fast and deadly his move had been just a little while before, Clint said, "I can believe that."

"Actually," Barton said, "that felt pretty good, you know? For the first time in a long time— since I lost my sight—I felt like I . . . I was worth something to somebody."

"Just my life, Stan," Clint said, "just my life."

"Yeah," Barton said.

They took a few moments to finish their beers, alone with their own thoughts, and then Clint set his empty mug down with a bang.

"It's time to find someplace to hole up ourselves," he said. "Someplace where we can watch the street from."

"The hotel seems to be the logical place," Barton said, "if it overlooks the street."

"It does," Clint said, "both rooms. We'll pick one and stay inside."

"What will we do for food?"

"There's plenty of food on the stove in the kitchen," Clint said. "I'll just take the whole pot of beef stew. Even cold it should be good."

"And beer?"

"There are probably some buckets in the kitchen," Clint said. "I'll fill them."

"Let's get it done, then," Barton said, getting to his feet. "They could come riding into town at any moment."

Chapter Forty

Clint took Barton back to the hotel room along with the pot of beef stew, then went back out to get the buckets of beer. He also made sure they had enough pillows and blankets, and ammunition for their pistols and rifles. He found it odd that he was thinking of keeping Barton's guns loaded as well, but the man had already proven the wisdom of that, hadn't he?

Crossing the street back to the hotel Clint still couldn't believe what had happened in the saloon. He'd never been that careless before, and if it hadn't been for Barton—a blind man!—he'd be a memory now.

Amazing.

Clint chose Barton's room for them to hole up in. It had just a little better view of the buildings across the street.

"You know, I had a thought," Barton said as Clint set up a chair by the window.

"About what?"

"About what they'll do when they come to town."

"Like what?"

"Well, somebody will take the horses to the livery . . ." Barton said.

"Right."

"And somebody will go into the saloon . . ."

"Uh-huh."

"And somebody will go looking for the old man . . ."

"Right."

"And," Barton said, "somebody will come here to make sure the rooms are ready."

Clint turned his head and looked at the blind man.

"If there are only three of them," Barton went on, "then they'll only need three rooms, but if there are more than three . . ."

"Then we're going to need to get out of here quickly," Clint finished.

"Right."

Clint turned in his chair to face Barton.

"I'd better check this place for a back door," he said. "Make sure we have a way out."

"Right," Barton said, "go ahead. I'll stand watch by the window."

"Stan—"

"Clint," he said, "if you open the window, I'll be able to hear if horses come riding down the street."

"Oh," Clint said, feeling dumb, "uh, yeah, that's right. Okay then."

He cracked the window and then vacated the chair so Barton could sit.

"I'll be right back."

"I'll be here," Barton said.

As Clint went out the door, Barton reached for the window, found it, and opened it wider so he could not only hear, but have the breeze on his face as well.

If they rode into town, he thought, and he started firing toward the sound, would he hit anyone? That was stupid. What if it was just some drifter riding in?

He had to face facts. Despite what had happened in the saloon, he was mostly useless. He was going to have to come to terms with that when this was all over and try to go on with his life.

And if he couldn't go on with his life—well, he could always end it, couldn't he?

Suicide.

The coward's way out.

Well, hell, who did he have to impress, anyway? There was no one left, not with Martha and Jimmy gone.

What was the difference if one more blind man, more or less, was alive or dead?

Clint went downstairs to the lobby and saw a curtained doorway right behind the desk. He had to go around the desk to get to it, then he found himself in a long hallway. He followed it all the way to the back, where it hooked up with another hallway. That one led to a door that took him outside.

He found a second set of steps back there which led up to the second floor, where he and Barton would be. This was good, it gave them a quick way out. Down the stairs, out the back, and over to the feed and grain where he had stashed the horses. All they'd have to carry with them were their guns and their saddlebags.

Of course, the escape route would only be necessary if the men who came to town were *not* the three Barton wanted, or if they had other men with them.

For a moment he sat on the steps and wondered how long they should wait. What if no one showed up for days? Should they still wait? Weeks? He supposed that would be up to Barton. After all, it was his vengeance they were in search of, wasn't it?

He turned and went up the stairs to rejoin Barton in the room.

Upstairs Stan Barton was thinking about John Running Deer. He was wondering how the old heathen was doing, and how things would be different if he was along. Would they be here? Or would they have taken a different route? Riding with Clint Adams was certainly different from riding with Running Deer. Running Deer had been with him from the beginning, but he wasn't sure at this point that he'd rather have the Indian with him than Clint Adams. After all, Clint was the man with the uncanny abilities with a gun. John Running Deer was adequate with a handgun and not bad with a rifle, but he didn't come close to the Gunsmith.

Of course, he himself had been excellent with both before he'd lost his sight. If he could see— well, then it wouldn't matter who he was with, Clint or John Running Deer. There wouldn't be any three men two of them couldn't handle successfully.

The way he was now, though, it was probably good that Clint Adams was along. Clint would have a chance facing three men—*any* three men. How well would John Running Deer fare in the same situation?

He was starting to wonder where Clint was when suddenly he heard something. He sat as still as the dead and strained to hear, leaning closer to the window.

Yes, there it was. He was certain.

The sound of horses.

Someone was coming.

Where was Clint?

Chapter Forty-One

How many?

He strained further, trying to hear how many different horses there were.

He became aware of footsteps coming down the hallway. It had to be Clint, because the riders hadn't arrived yet. Still, what if they had sent someone ahead to check things out?

The door opened, and he drew his gun and pointed. . . .

Clint moved down the hall quickly, uneasy at having left Barton alone. No matter how he seemed, the man had been unnerved by the incident in the saloon. It had probably been the first time he'd fired his gun—other than in practice—since he'd lost his sight.

Clint opened the door and entered the room, saw Barton draw his gun, turn, and point. . . .

"Take it easy!" he said. "It's me."

"Jesus," Barton said, putting up his gun. "Clint, I hear horses."

"Move!" Clint said.

Barton got out of the chair, groped behind him for the bed, and sat on it as Clint moved to the window.

Clint looked out the window just as the riders came into view. He watched, and counted.

Two . . .

Three . . .

And two more . . .

"Five," he said to Barton, "there are five of them, Stan."

"Could be worse," Barton said. "Can you see their faces?"

"No," Clint said. "They've stopped in front of the saloon."

"What are they doing?"

"Quiet."

Clint watched as the five men dismounted, talking among themselves. A couple of them turned their heads and looked around, maybe looking for Emory, the old man.

They talked a few moments longer, pointing. One man in particular seemed to be doing the most talking, a big man wearing a black Stetson. He seemed to be the boss. Maybe he was divvying up the responsibilities, Clint thought. . . . Yes, one of the men was taking the reins of all five horses, and another was going into the saloon. If they only went as far as the saloon, they wouldn't find the body, yet, and Clint had left some of the food on the stove.

"Wha—" Barton started, but Clint turned and cut him off.

"I have an idea, Stan."

"What?"

"One man is taking the horses to the livery," Clint said. "If I can get there . . ."

Barton knew what he meant. If he could get there and surprise him, that would be one less man they'd have to deal with.

"Stay in this room," Clint said.

"Where would I go?" the blind man asked.

As Clint went to the door and opened it, Barton said, "Sing out when you come back, otherwise I'm opening fire as soon as the door opens."

"Good idea," Clint said. "I'll be back as soon as I can."

Yeah, Stan Barton thought as Clint went out, with a little luck.

Clint ran down the back stairs and out the back door. Leaving Barton alone was taking a big chance—as was his acting on impulse this way. Once he took the first man out of the play there would be no turning back, even if they *weren't* the men Barton was looking for.

Still, it was better to be doing *something*. . . .

Chapter Forty-Two

Clint stayed off the main street, choosing instead to run behind the buildings and through alleys. When he finally did have to come out onto the street it was far enough away from the saloon that he wouldn't be seen. Still, he stayed close to the abandoned storefronts as he made his way to the livery.

When he reached the livery, he moved toward the front doors and peered inside. As he did so, he heard a man talking.

". . . think I am . . ." he was saying, "son of a bitch, goddamn it, always got to be the one who takes care of the horses. . . ."

The man kept up his complaining as he was unsaddling the horses. Two were done, and he was working on the third. His work, and his talking, would keep him from hearing Clint moving up behind him.

Clint slipped into the livery and drew his gun. He hated using his gun to hit people on the head with. You might come upon someone with a head hard enough to damage the weapon, but he didn't have much choice here.

The man was unsaddling the fourth horse when Clint came up behind him and brought the handle of his gun down on the fellow's head. The man slumped to the ground, out cold. Clint holstered his gun and grabbed a rope off one of the horses to tie him up with. He used the man's own bandanna to gag him with.

When he was finished tying the man up, he turned him over so he could get a good look at his face. He did not fit Barton's description of any of the three men who had shot his family.

Hastily Clint went through the man's pockets, but all he found was four bits and some lint.

He checked the man's bonds one more time before he left, wanting to make sure he wasn't able to get lose.

As he left the livery stable he thought, one down, four to go.

Stan Barton was frightened.

For the first time in his life he was truly scared. This was the first time he'd been in a dangerous situation since he'd been blinded. He had never realized before how truly frightening it would be to be in the dark at a time like this. Even if Clint succeeded in taking one man out of the play, there were still four outlaws—maybe killers—walking around town, and he couldn't see!

He sat with his back against the bedpost, his gun held in both hands pointed directly ahead of him. What if he wasn't pointing right at the door? What if he was pointing his gun at a wall, and somebody came through the door? He'd pull the trigger, again and again, emptying his gun at a wall and before he knew it, from out of the darkness, a bullet would come smashing into him, killing him.

Well, what of it? he thought as a bead of sweat dripped off the end of his nose. He'd be dead then. What would be so bad about that? No more dreams, no more fear of the dark. . . .

Jesus, he thought, would he be blind in the Hereafter if he died now?

Clint made his way back to the hotel by the same route. He had left the back door ajar, and now he went up the rear steps and went back down the hall to the room where he'd left Stan Barton.

"Stan!" he said at the door, trying not to be too loud, yet still loud enough for the man to hear him. "Stan, it's me!"

"Come ahead."

Clint entered the room and saw Barton sitting on the bed with his gun held in both hands, pointed right at the door.

"Take it easy, Stan."

"Jesus," Barton said, letting the barrel of the gun droop, "I thought you were never coming back. You were gone for hours."

"Stan," Clint said, "I was only gone about twenty minutes."

"Well, it seemed like an hour," Barton said. "What happened?"

"I got one of them trussed up at the livery stable," Clint said. "that leaves four."

"Was he one of them?" the blind man asked.

"No, Stan, he wasn't."

"Damn it, Clint!" Barton said. "Tell me the truth. Was he?"

"Calm down, Stan," Clint said, going to the window. "I am telling you the truth. He didn't fit any of the descriptions you gave me."

"Damn," Barton muttered.

Clint looked out the window at the front of the saloon. The four of them were probably inside. He wondered if they had found Emory's body yet. Surely they'd seen the mess behind the bar. What would they think of that?

"Did you hear anyone come into the hotel while I was gone?" he asked.

"No," Barton said, "I didn't hear anything."

"Well, the window was open," Clint said. "You might have heard something if they'd come across. They must be in the saloon, eating and drinking."

"If they find the old man's body—"

"If they do that," Clint said, "they'll be looking for us next."

"So what do we do?"

"We're going to have to go looking for them, instead," Clint said.

"That means you."

"I know."

"I feel so helpless!"

Clint looked at him. This might have been the first time he really felt sorry for Stan Barton.

"You weren't helpless in the saloon earlier today," Clint said.

"That was luck," Barton said, "a whole lot of luck."

"Okay," Clint said, "so it was luck. All we need is for the luck to run a little longer."

"What are you going to do?" Barton asked.

"I've got to go down there and get the drop on them," Clint said. "I'll try to get into the saloon through the back. When I have them, I'll call out to you, just to let you know, but stay up here, all right?"

"Sure," Barton said, "sure, I will."

Chapter Forty-Three

Clint left the hotel, again by the back door, again worried at leaving the blind man alone. If this worked, though, he'd be able to get the drop on all four of the remaining men at one time. What would remain then was simply to find out who they were, and what they were wanted for. That is, if they were not the men Stan Barton was searching for.

He took a roundabout route, once again using alleys, until he could cross the street to the saloon and the alley that ran alongside it. He worked his way toward the back of the saloon, hoping that there would be a way in.

In the alley he paused to look in a window, and he saw four men sitting at a table eating. How long, he thought, before they miss the fifth man?

They were eating and drinking beer and apparently not worried about the mess behind the bar. From his vantage point, he could see two of their faces, and neither man fit the descriptions given him by Stan Barton.

That left the other two men, sitting with their backs to him, as possibilities.

He continued to the end of the alley and on behind the saloon, where he found a back door. If it was locked he was going to have to try to force it quietly. Luckily, when he turned the doorknob the door opened easily. He entered, closing the door behind him. Once inside, he could hear the drone of voices.

He had two ways to go, left or right. He went right, came to another hallway. When he looked down it, he saw Emory's body lying on the floor. That meant that this hallway led to the kitchen. He reversed direction. The voices became louder, and soon he came to a doorway that led into the saloon. He peered out and saw the table where the men were sitting.

He backed up, took out his gun, then stepped out of the doorway, pointing it.

"Hold it right there!"

The men froze and looked at him.

All three of them.

Three?

Where was the fourth man?

"Just stand easy," Clint said, moving closer to them. "Where's the other one?"

"What other one?" one of the men asked.

He could see all three of their faces now, and none of them matched the descriptions given him by Stan Barton.

"All right," Clint said, taking a quick look around, "I'll have to settle for three of you."

"Who are you, mister?" one of the other ones asked.

"I'm the fella who has the drop on you, that's who," Clint said. "Take your guns out and toss them away."

"Look, mister, we ain't done nothin'—"

"Just do it!"

Two of the men looked at the third one, who nodded, and they all dropped their guns on the floor.

"Okay, that's good," Clint said, moving even closer.

Now what was he supposed to do? What if the other man went over to the hotel for some reason? He had to immobilize these men so he could find the fourth one and check on Barton.

"Okay," he said, "you're going to tie each other up."

"Wait—"

"We need some rope," Clint said, looking around. "Maybe in the kitchen—"

"Ain't no rope in the kitchen," a voice said behind him.

Clint froze.

"Just stand easy, fella," the voice said. "Drop the gun to the floor, like you made my friends do."

Clint did as he was told.

The man came into view then, moving so that he was standing with his back to the batwing doors.

Clint looked at the man and saw that he had a scar across his face, from the bottom of his left eye across the bridge of his nose to the corner of his mouth.

"Suppose you tell us who you are and what you think you're doin'," the man said.

"I just thought we'd get acquainted."

"Wait a minute," one of the other men said. He had blond hair and a blond mustache. "Where's Sam? What did you do with Sam?"

"If he's the one you sent to the livery stable, he's fine. I just tied him up."

"He's my brother," the man said. "You better be tellin' the truth."

"Never mind that," Scarface said. "Who are you, mister?"

"My name's Clint Adams."

"No kidding?" one of the other men said. He was about twenty and very thin.

"No kidding," Clint said.

"Hey," the kid said, "he's famous. He's the Gunsmith."

"We know who he is, kid," Scarface said.

"What we want to know," Blondie said, "is what he's doin' here."

"Before we kill him," Scarface said.

"Well," Clint said, "if you're going to kill me, what's the difference?"

"You know something, Mr. Gunsmith?" Scarface said, raising his gun. "You're right."

Chapter Forty-Four

Stan Barton finally decided that he couldn't just stay in his room and wait for the sound of shots. He had to do something, even if he was blind. How hard could it be to find his way out of the room, down the hall, and down the stairs to the lobby? All he had to do was feel his way along.

He stood up and moved toward the door, imagining where it must be. He found it, turned the knob, and stepped out into the hall. Once there he tried to remember which way they had come from. He turned left and groped for the opposite wall. If he was right he should come to the stairs . . . there they were. Now all he had to do was feel for the banister, grab it, and take the steps one at a time.

All right, he was in the lobby. The front door was open; he could feel a breeze coming in. He followed his senses and eventually found his way to the door.

Good. He was at the front of the hotel. Now

what was he supposed to do? How could he find the saloon?

He tried to remember how Clint had described the scene to him when they arrived. He said that there were three buildings on each side of the street that had been kept up. The hotel, Clint had said, was the center building on this side.

Now he tried to remember when they had walked across the street to the saloon. Yes, that was right, Clint had said that the saloon was the building on the left. They had gone across the street diagonally. All he had to do was follow the same route . . . and he'd be out in the open, in the middle of the street. There could have been dozens of people watching him, and he'd never know.

Still, he couldn't just wait. He had to do something.

He took a deep breath and stepped out of the hotel. Feeling with his foot he found the step down into the street. When he had both feet in the street he started across diagonally, keeping his hands stretched out in front of him. He felt very open, very naked, but he insisted on going on. Eventually, he started to hear voices and follow them. The voices, he decided, would lead him right to the saloon.

And then he heard Clint's voice, loud and commanding—and he bumped into the boardwalk, almost tripping and falling. He was there, across the street, and from the sound of the voices he was right outside the saloon. He stepped up onto the walk and, using his ears, his hands outstretched, began to look for the front entrance . . . and then he heard another voice.

"Just stand easy, fella," he heard the voice say, and then the man told Clint to drop his gun. Barton actually heard Clint's gun hit the floor.

He touched a wall and started to feel for the batwing doors, listening to the conversation inside. Clint wouldn't say anything about him, he knew. In fact, he wouldn't answer any questions.

" . . . what's the difference?" he heard Clint say.

"You know something, Mr. Gunsmith?" he heard the other voice say. "You're right."

And then he touched the batwing doors. He was there, at the entrance!

But what could he do?

Suddenly, Clint saw Barton at the doorway. The blind man had his gun out.

Don't come in, Clint thought, don't . . .

Barton stepped into the room.

"Hold it!" he shouted.

The three men at the table looked at Barton. If they noticed that he was blind . . .

The scar-faced man couldn't look at Barton directly, however, and he was the only one holding a gun. The others had not picked theirs up yet.

"Drop the gun," Barton said to Scarface.

Scarface had to keep his eyes on Clint, his gun pointed right at him.

"You shoot me," he said, "I'll pull the trigger and plug your friend. Drop *your* gun."

"I think we'll take that chance," Barton said. "If I drop my gun, you'll kill us both. At least this way, I take you down, too."

Clint wasn't watching Barton or Scarface. He was watching the blond man, who was looking at Barton intently. If he noticed that Barton was blind and said something . . . Clint looked down at his gun on the floor at his feet. He was going to have to make a move.

"I said drop it!" Barton said.

Scarface was undecided, and then Blondie spoke.

"Hey, wait a minute," he said. "Jesus, he's blind! He can't see!"

"What?" Scarface said.

Clint dropped to the floor as Scarface turned around to face Barton.

"Fire, Stan, fire!" Clint shouted.

The other three men went for their guns.

Barton pulled the trigger of his gun, again and again.

Clint grabbed his and began firing.

Barton missed the scar-faced man completely, but one of his bullets caught one of the other men, the blond one. Clint fired, his bullet striking a second man, killing him instantly.

The scar-faced man hit the floor and aimed his gun at Barton, who was still pulling his trigger, dropping the hammer on his empty cylinders.

Clint shot Scarface in the back, to save Barton. Meanwhile, the other man fired at Clint, winging him in the left arm. Clint spun around and fired again, killing the fourth man.

"Clint! Clint!" Barton shouted when the shooting stopped. "What's happening? Are you all right?"

"I'm hit," Clint said, "but I'm all right. What about you?"

Barton felt his body with his free hand and said, "I don't seem to be shot."

"Good."

"What about the others?"

"There are four of them, Stan," Clint said. "They're dead. I got three, you got one."

"I got one?"

"Yeah, you did."

"Are any of them . . . ?"

"Yes, Stan," Clint said. "The man with the scar is here."

Barton's face turned pale.

"Where is he? Where? Take me to him!"

Clint holstered his gun and walked across the room to Barton. He took the man by the elbow and led him to the dead man with the scar.

"He's at your feet."

"Right at my feet?"

"Yes."

And suddenly Barton was kicking the dead man, again and again, and tears were streaming down his face. Abruptly, he fell to his knees next to the man, felt for him, and began pummeling him with his fists. Tears were still coming, but he wasn't making any sound beyond grunting with the effort of hitting him.

Clint decided that was enough. He moved around behind Barton and put his arms around him, pinning the man's arms to his side. He pulled him away from the dead man.

"That's enough, Stan," he said, over and over again, "that's enough."

Barton struggled for a few moments, then stopped. He became deadweight in Clint's arms.

"What about the others?" he asked weakly. "Are any of them . . . ?"

"No," Clint said, "none of the rest match the descriptions. This one must have split from the others."

"Tell me," Barton said, "tell me which one I killed, Clint."

He had killed the blond man, but Clint said, "You killed him, Stan. You killed the man with the scar."

"Thank God," Barton said, "thank God. . . ."

Chapter Forty-Five

They went to the livery to question the fifth man in the hope that he could tell them where the other men were, the others who had killed Stan Barton's family. When they got to the stable, though, they found the man a bloody mess, dead. Apparently, one or more of the horses had trampled him for some reason . . . stomped him to death.

"We'll get nothing out of him," Clint said. "I'm sorry, Stan."

"Don't be sorry," Barton said. "You've helped me a lot, Clint. I got one of the men. I got him!"

"Yes, you did," Clint said. "And now you'll want to find the others."

"Yes," Barton said, "yes, I will . . . but not with you."

"What?"

"I can't ask you to ride with me anymore, Clint," Barton said. "This is not your fight."

"Stan—"

"No, I'm serious," Barton said. "When we get to the next town, I'll telegraph John Running Deer and I'll wait there for him."

"But the trail—"

"The trail is cold," Barton said. "This was probably the gang we heard about, and now they're all dead. The trail is cold. I'll wait for John, and we'll try to find a new trail. You have no . . . debt to me, Clint Adams. I have a debt to you, though, a debt I'll someday pay."

Clint put his hand on Barton's arm.

"I'll go and get our gear and bring it back here," Clint said. "We'll saddle up and leave."

"Okay," Barton said. "I'll wait here."

Clint started to walk out, then turned and said, "I hope things work out for you, Stan. I really do."

"Yeah," Stan Barton said, "I hope so, too."

Clint left Barton in the livery, left the man alone with his first taste of vengeance. Would he like it? Clint didn't know. He knew, though, that Barton wouldn't quit until he found the other men and killed them, too . . . and then what?

What would the blind ex-lawman do then?

ANGEL EYES *series*
by
Award-Winning Author
Robert J. Randisi (J.R. Roberts)

Visit us at www.speakingvolumes.us

TRACKER *series*
by
Award-Winning Author
Robert J. Randisi (J.R. Roberts)

Visit us at www.speakingvolumes.us

MOUNTAIN JACK PIKE *series*
by
Award-Winning Author
Robert J. Randisi (J.R. Roberts)

Visit us at www.speakingvolumes.us

Sign up for free and bargain books

Join the Speaking Volumes mailing list

Text
ILOVEBOOKS
to 22828 to get started.